Shashi Deshpande was born in Dharwad, India, daughter
of the renowned dramatist and Sanskrit scholar, Shriranga.
At the age of fifteen she went to Bombay, graduated in
Economics, then moved to Bangalore, where she gained a
degree in Law. The early years of her marriage were
largely given over to the care of her two young sons, but
she took a course in journalism and for a time worked on a
magazine. Her writing career only began in earnest in 1970,
initially with short stories, of which several volumes have
been published. She is also the author of four children's
books and five previous novels – *The Dark Holds No
Terrors, If I Die Today, Come Up and Be Dead, Roots and
Shadows* and *That Long Silence* (Virago, 1988), which won
the Sahilya Akademi award and has been widely translated.
Shashi Deshpande lives in Bangalore with her pathologist
husband.

The
Binding Vine

Shashi Deshpande

Published by VIRAGO PRESS Limited, 1993
20–23 Mandela Street, Camden Town, London NW1 0HQ

*A CIP catalogue record for this book is available
from the British Library*

Printed in Britain by Cox & Wyman Ltd, Reading, Berks.

ACKNOWLEDGEMENTS

I have to acknowledge my debt to my late friend Anupama Niranjana, for reading and discussing this novel while I was writing it, and for her constant encouragement, even in the last stages of her terminal illness.

My thanks to Githa Hariharan for giving the novel a brilliantly perceptive once-over; to Professor P. Lal, for so kindly allowing me to use his words from his transcreation of the *Mahabharata* on p. 202; to my husband for, as always, being my first reader; and, above all, to Pratibha Nandakumar for her generous and enthusiastic help in creating Mira's poems, which, until then, had seemed impossible.

'What were the use of my creation, if I were entirely contained here?'

Emily Brontë
Wuthering Heights

PART ONE

The fragrance of the night-queen
crosses the hedge of thorns
touches the pinnacle of the shrine
and is no longer mine.

We all of us grow up with an idea of ourselves, an image rather, and spend the rest of our lives trying to live up to it. But for me, I suddenly realise as Vanaa talks to me, it's been a constant struggle against an image of myself imposed upon me by Vanaa.

'Do you remember, Urmi, how you once fell off a bike when you were learning to ride?'

'Once? I must have fallen at least a dozen times.'

'Yes, but this was a particularly bad fall. You hadn't yet learnt to balance yourself properly. I was holding the bike to steady you and you kept yelling at me to let go. "I can manage," you kept screaming. So I let go . . .'

And, pedalling furiously, I lost control and crashed on a pile of stones by the roadside.

'Yes, I remember that. I still have the scars.'

'It was ghastly – both your knees were terribly gashed. We tried pressing your skirt on them to stanch the blood, but in a minute your skirt was red.'

She stops, looks at me, waiting perhaps for me to say something, then goes on.

'You couldn't walk properly, you hobbled, but you were more concerned with your wheels being out of alignment; you wanted to straighten them out. And when we went to your Baiajji, the first thing you said to her was "I'm not going to stop cycling, Baiajji, I'm not going to stop".' Again she pauses.

'Well, what are you trying to say?' She continues to gaze at me helplessly. 'Why don't you say it straight off, Vanaa? I know what you're trying to tell me. But that was just a hurt, a small hurt, and this is my child, Vanaa, it's my child.'

'I know, I didn't mean . . .'

She can't go on. In the silence that falls between us the thought comes to me that I've always had a sense of being privileged, that it's Vanaa who made me feel this way.

'*Hubris*.' The word comes out loud. Vanaa gives me a startled look. 'Now I know what it is. Yes, it's right I should suffer.'

'Urmi, that's morbid. What do you mean?'

'I had too much, don't you see? That's why I had to lose Anu.'

'You're talking nonsense, Urmi. This isn't like you.'

'But Vanaa, it was you who made me feel that, you who said it to me, that I had too much.'

'I did? I can't remember.'

'Well, maybe you didn't use those exact words, but that's what you meant. I can remember how indignant I was. I felt you were accusing me of a wrong and I had to do something to put it right. You remember all the clothes Inni used to get me – those smart frocks, skirts and jeans? I managed never to wear them, remember?'

'I can remember what you did wear – God, those awful clothes your grandmother stitched for you!'

'I preferred them. Inni's clothes made me feel I was different.'

8

'You looked different all right in your Baiajji's clothes. You must have been the worst dressed child in school.'

'I didn't mind that. It was better than being distinctive in Inni's expensive clothes. That's why I kept on wearing the things Baiajji stitched – however old or shabby they got. I made her let them out until there was nothing to let out. And Inni's dresses stayed in the cupboard until I could say – truthfully – that they were too small for me.'

Vanaa's face is troubled. 'Urmi, I think you're making too much of something I said as a child. And we were friends, Urmi. Surely I would never have said that.'

'You know, Vanaa, the funniest thing is that we were not well off at all – my grandparents, I mean. Oh, they were not poverty-stricken, I don't mean that. But for Aju there was only his pension and it wasn't very much. In fact Papa was horrified when he found out, after Aju's death, what his bank balance was. It was just a façade of splendour.'

'But the house, Urmi, the house . . .'

'Yes, even the house, it was the same, wasn't it. Only a splendid façade. Remember how it was inside, Vanaa? None of the rooms matched the outside, except the durbar hall.'

'It was grand,' she says, unwilling to let go her idea of the house. Her face is admiring and wistful and it reminds me of the child Vanaa, saying to me the first time I took her home, 'You live here? In this house?'

There can be no vaulting over time. We have to walk every step of the way, however difficult or painful it is; we can avoid nothing. And I have no desire to leap into the future, either, to project myself into a time when all this pain will be a thing of the past, healed and forgotten. This pain is all that's left to me of Anu. Without it, there will be nothing left to me of her; I will lose her entirely.

But I can escape into the past. Vanaa's face, when she speaks of the Ranidurg house, as if she is seeing it as a child, takes me back there and I can see it myself, not diminished and dingy as it seems now, but the way it was to me when I was a child. I have to raise my head to take it in, the porch with its lofty pillars, the buttressed terrace above, the huge front door with large canopied windows on either side. I quail at the thought of entering the house through the front door; we never do that, but this one time I will. With an effort I push the heavy door open and enter the small drab hall, which is merely the prelude to the grandeur of the durbar hall. It is Papa who calls it that, with a smile on his face; but to me it is truly magnificent. It subdues me with its size, its high-raftered ceiling, panelled walls and fireplace, its polished black and white tiled floor, and the chandelier – above all the chandelier.

We come into this room, Baiajji and I, once a month to clean it. We open all the windows before we begin and the breeze sets the chandelier tinkling.

'Listen, Baiajji, listen,' I appeal to her. She strains to hear, her head cocked, her face screwed up in concentration. And there it is, a small, infinitely musical tinkle. We smile at each other and go back to our work.

I am allowed to help. I clamber up a chair to get down the photographs of the Raja and his Rani from the mantelpiece. As I begin to dust them Baiajji warns me, 'Be careful with those gods'. She smiles, the way Papa does when he says 'durbar hall'. And I will know only much later, that they are both making gentle fun of Aju's exaggerated reverence for the Raja who gifted him this house in a burst of generosity when his son, whom Aju tutored, graduated.

Nothing else interests me here, neither Papa's and Inni's bedroom – though I linger for a moment, fascinated by a trace of Inni's perfume which seems to have stayed behind – nor the large dining room which is never used. I am eager to get into our domain, the new extension, which is where my grandparents and I really live. There is a faint quiver in

10

me as I run through the long dark corridor which links the two parts of the house, as if the horror of the future is crouching somewhere in a dark corner. It is a relief to be in our familiar hall with its shabby, sagging sofa and the ancient GEC radio enshrined on a high table. But it is in the dining room that we spend most of our time, Baiajji and I; the table is always littered with my school books, Baiajji's letters and the bits of paper on which she does her accounts.

Now there are two doors before me, absolutely identical, except for a paper stuck on one door which says 'Baiajji's and Urmila's room'. I have written this and Amrut has added 'and Amurts', squeezing the letters into the little space left. The rooms behind the doors are two halves of a large rectangular room, divided by a wooden partition running along its length. Aju's room is neat and dull, there is nothing interesting here, except the large globe, a relic of his teaching days. Baiajji's and my room, though the same size as Aju's, is so cluttered it looks much smaller. And chaotic. But it isn't. Nothing is ever moved from its place. Baiajji and I never have to search for anything, we can find things even in the dark.

The furniture, however, leads a peripatetic existence. Baiajji has a craze for moving things, and when I wake up I never know where I am. Sometimes I am facing the wall, sometimes the wooden partition, from behind which I can hear the faint sounds of Aju coughing and moving about, and some mornings I wake up to see a bit of the sky through the branches of the neem tree. But there is never any disorientation, because always by my side there is Baiajji's bed, already neatly made, the blanket folded into a square at the foot of it.

I go into the garden and there she is, squatting before a freshly-planted mango sapling, her two assistants standing before her with an air of resignation, while she harangues them about something. They nod their heads, seeming to

11

agree with everything she says, but we know they will go on doing things their own way.

'Don't go near the tamarind trees,' Baiajji calls after me as, bored with them, I run off. I don't bother to reply. There is no time when the tamarind trees do not hold temptation for us. We eat the tender green leaves, the crisp white and yellow flowers, the tiny curving fruits that emerge from the flowers, each pod delicately outlined like a baby's fingers, and then the larger, raw tamarinds that even when seasoned with salt and chilli powder, set our teeth on edge with their sourness. But now, when they are ripe and most tempting, the trees are out of bounds. They are guarded by the man who has bought them off Aju, and we are not allowed near them.

It is time for the train, anyway, so I run to the front of the house, nimbly avoiding the tufts of thick, thorny grass and, digging my toes into the grooves in the wall, climb up. It is always a moment of exquisite happiness to sit up here and look down on the railway lines shimmering in the sunlight. I can hear the distant, melancholy whistle of the train and excitement begins building in me. It is climbing the gradient – puff puff – it sounds like a creature in distress – puff puff – it is exhausted – puff puff – and now, in a sudden burst of energy, it is over the gradient. There is a triumphant, strident whistle – HERE I AM. I can see it now, I can hear the clickety clackety of the wheels. Some of the passengers wave at me, but I don't respond, I never do; I am intent on watching the rails. It seems like a miracle to me, to see them emerge unscathed from the pounding they take as the train passes over them. As it goes round the curve – carriage by carriage it slides sinuously past it – I watch breathlessly: what if the rails finally succumb and the carriages topple over? But no, the last bit of it disappears, leaving a kind of thundering trapped in the rails,

12

a humming in the wires overhead. And the unmistakable stench of railway toilets.

Tired of being alone, I decide to go to Vanaa's house. I run to the side of the house, where a thick hedge separates our house from theirs. I run up and down, looking for the gap in the hedge through which we run all day; but there is nothing, no gap, no hedge either, only a blank wall, glass-topped, the glass bits shining menacingly in the sunlight. My exit is barred. I can't go back, I am trapped in the present. There is no escape. I put my head on my knees and let the agony come through.

Perhaps it is another time, or another day, I don't know. The days merge into one another. Vanaa is once again with me. It looks like they're frightened of me, they don't want to leave me alone. But why is it always Vanaa? And how long has she been here? I notice her only when she makes a small sound, it's like a timid nudge, to draw attention to herself. Yet the moment I see her she looks apprehensive. Is she scared of me? I wish they'd realise that it makes no difference to me, whether I'm alone or whether someone is with me.

Suddenly, as if she can't bear the silence any more, Vanaa bursts out, 'Talk! Say something! Why don't you say something?'

'What?'

'Anything. Just speak. Don't keep it bottled within you. Why don't you cry, Urmi? It's unnatural not to cry.'

'Really, Vanaa, you're getting hysterical. It's absurd. You should be telling me not to cry. And why are you crying? Do you think that helps me?'

'I can't bear it.'

'That's plain stupid. What do you have to bear?'

'It's all my fault. You know you're thinking it – you have been thinking it. Why don't you say it aloud?'

'Please Vanaa, stop this nonsense.'

'It isn't nonsense. If I hadn't taken Anu away with me, if I hadn't . . .'

'If I hadn't, if you hadn't – it's all so futile, this kind of thinking. It would have happened anyway. You're a doctor's wife, you should know that.'

'But you could have been with her.'

'That wouldn't have made any difference to Anu, would it? It's nobody's fault, Vanaa. It's no use doing these – post mortems . . .'

'Urmi . . .'

'Vanaa, please leave me alone.'

'Urmi, I can't bear to see your pain.'

'Don't see it then. Go away and leave me alone. Why don't you all leave me alone? Do you think it helps to have you watching me all the time?'

'Urmi . . .'

'Go away, Vanaa, just go away.'

The silence is restful. There are no sounds except for the tick tock of a timepiece. And the beating of my heart. I remember the sound of Anu's heart beating, her breathing. I knew the exact moment she died; I heard her expel her breath – a loud harsh sound that tore into me. Then all the tumult died down and there was silence. In a moment, the cushioning left me and the terrible certainty of her death came to me. No, I must not think of this now, I must not . . .

A sound seeps through the silence in the flat. The sound of someone crying in the next room. Vanaa always cries easily, but these racking sobs begin to irritate me. 'I can't bear your pain.' Why can't I feel her pain? Why can't I feel anyone's pain? Kishore lying beside me in bed, his arms by his sides, his profile sharp and clear as always, and the tears pouring down his face. When was this? The night after Anu's death? I could have wiped his tears, but I didn't. I watched with a detached curiosity instead. How could a

14

person cry so soundlessly? And now Vanaa. Has Anu taken all my capacity to feel away with her? I begin to bang my head against the wall. I can hear the dull rhythmic thud thud. There's nothing else. No pain at all.

'What are you doing, Urmi? What are you doing?'

Vanaa is holding my shoulders in a frenzied grip, so tight that I cannot move. I look up and I can see both of us in the mirror across the room. There is a small, angry bump on my forehead, a needle-long, needle-thin cut in the centre of it. It looks as if it has deliberately closed up, refusing to let the blood come through. I can feel a tight drumming at the point. No pain, even now, just that tight drumming, as if the blood is knocking there, impatient to be let out.

'I was banging my head against the wall,' I tell Vanaa matter-of-factly.

Vanaa is breathing hard, like a person who has been running. She stares at me in silence.

'And look, I can't even bleed.'

I move away from under Vanaa's hands. I have to wrench my shoulder away from the tight hold. Her hands stay for a while in the air, shaped to the grip, then she walks out of the room.

'Hurt yourself?' Amrut comes in and casually asks me.

'Not really.'

'Let's have a look. You're right, it's only a scratch. Still . . . Mandira, get me some ice cubes.'

'What happened Amrutmama? Let me see what happened.'

'Nothing. Urmi's hurt herself. It's all right Inni, nothing to make a fuss about. Just send some ice cubes with Mandira.'

We sit in silence until the child returns with a bowl of ice cubes.

'Does that hurt?'

'Yes.'

15

But the truth is that there's still nothing. No pain.

'Urmiauntie, is it paining a lot?'

'No Mandira, not very much.'

'Then why are you crying?'

'Ssh Mandira, don't jabber. Just hold this here – like this. Don't let go, mind. I'll get some Dettol.'

'No Amrut, it's okay, there's no need to fuss. I'd like to lie down for a while.'

'Right then. Come on, Mandira, out we go.'

I am running along the sea. There's someone else with me – a someone who is running beside me. I can hear the footsteps, I can hear the heavy breathing, but I cannot see whoever it is. Nor can I see the sea. Like the person beside me, I only know it is there, outside the range of my vision. I have to keep running, and I go on, looking straight ahead, the invisible person keeping pace with me. Now it is becoming difficult; the sand, soft and squishy under my feet, keeps dragging me down. Each time it is getting harder and harder to pull my feet out of the bog-like softness. I labour on, the person beside me panting louder and louder too. I can't go on . . . I can't go . . .

I wake up. That was a dream. The room is dark. I can hear Kartik breathing. I must get back to sleep.

Now I am walking along a narrow dark corridor. I am passing Inni's room. Inni is awake, I can hear the sounds of her breathing. Yes, of course, Inni is doing her *Pranaayaam* – such loud snuffling sounds. Why is the blanket over my head? I am suffocating. I can't breathe . . .

I wake up once again. The sounds of breathing are my own. I am damp, perspiring, there is a ringing in my ears. I try to exhale, there is something, a weight on my chest. I must get rid of it, I have to . . .

'Kartik . . . Kartik . . .'

'Mama . . . ?'

16

'Kartik , I'm sick . . . call . . . someone . . .'

There are faces about me, Amrut bending over me, asking me something. Such a lot of light. Why is it so bright? I can't answer Amrut, I can only go on with my agonised struggle to breathe . . .

'Urmi . . .'

A loud voice penetrates. The face, even through the haze, is confident and reassuring.

'Urmi, relax. It's only an attack of asthma. I'll give you something. You'll be all right.'

It is like a miracle. The huge weight on my chest is easing, the constriction inside is dissolving. It is possible to breathe. Someone is wiping my face. I open my eyes and see Inni crying. I try to smile reassuringly, give it up and concentrate on breathing again. I slump, begin to slip down.

'Hey, Didi, sit up . Don't lie down Urmi, don't . . .'

Amrut's tone, his face are frantic. I smile at him. It is possible to do that now.

'I won't die.' The words come out loud and clear.

'Urmi . . .'

I open my eyes. It is Vanaa.

'Where the hell were you all this time?'

'Gosh, she's fine now.'

'Back to normal.'

Somebody laughs.

'Urmila,' it's Harish's voice, 'you'll go to sleep now, okay?'

I close my eyes and lie still, feeling my breath go out easily.

'How do you feel?'

Harish is sitting by me, looking down at me, a professional look on his face.

'Okay. But empty. As if the core of me has been scooped out, leaving a hollow.'

17

'You'll feel better after you've eaten something. No, don't smile, I know what you meant. And I still say eating will make you feel better.'

'Not for the kind of emptiness I have within me.'

'Well, you're depressed. That's only natural in your situation. But you'll be all right. And I'm not just saying it . . .'

'It's a professional prognosis. Right, Harish, I accept it.'

'Believe me, Urmi, I'm not trying to belittle your sorrow by talking clinically. I'm trying to tell you that this – losing a loved one – happens to every human. People recover eventually, don't they?'

'That doesn't comfort me very much. Not right now. How does it help me to know that others have suffered like me? But I know what you mean. I . . .' For a moment it is difficult to go on, 'I'm trying to come to terms with it, Harish.'

'We all know that.' It's his turn to hesitate now. 'Urmi, should we write to Kishore?'

'About me?' He nods. 'Is this a crisis? I mean, am I so ill that he has to rush back to me?'

'No, no, you know it isn't like that.'

'Then what's the point? You know he'd already over-stayed; he doesn't have any leave. And I'll be fine.'

'Spoken like a sailor's wife.'

'It was only an attack of asthma, wasn't it?'

'Of course. Inni says you used to get these attacks as a child.'

'She does? That's funny. I knew nothing about it.'

'You couldn't. You were too little. It was before you went to live in Ranidurg, she said.'

'Oh, maybe that's why . . . Anyway, it's over. It won't happen again, will it?'

'Hopefully not.'

'In that case don't say anything to Kishore. Tell Vanaa I'll write to him myself.'

18

'Okay, it's your decision. But you must get yourself into better shape. Physically, I mean.'

'I will. I'm tough. You know that.'

'Urmi, do you remember saying the word "anguish" during your attack? We couldn't quite make out what you were saying. It was Vanaa who finally got it.'

'Yes, I remember that.'

'Well, if that's what you're really suffering from, give your anguish to me. It'll keep. I'll give it back to you when you're strong enough to hold on to it.'

'Why, Harish, now I know why Vanaa married you!'

'You do? Good. Better late than never. I've always felt you didn't appreciate me.' He is smiling as he says this.

'I was jealous of you.'

'I never minded your place in Vanaa's life. I still don't. But when I see her tearing herself into pieces over you . . . like when you did this . . .' He gently touches my forehead. 'It's healing. Don't do this kind of thing again, will you?'

'I won't, I promise you I won't.'

'Don't do that kind of thing again.' Does he think I will? Yes, they all do. They think that it was an outburst of hysteria, that I was behaving like those women who beat at their breasts and tear their hair in their grief. Or do they think it's a sign of a breakdown? Yes, that's right, that's what they're afraid of, that's why they all watch me so carefully, so anxiously. That's why they want Kishore to be here – to pick up the bits and pieces. And put them together again? All the King's horses and all the King's men couldn't put Humpty-Dumpty together again. What's broken can't be mended. But I'm not broken, I'm not going to break.

'Mama, you won't die, will you?' Kartik asked me, his eyes on my face, intent on my answer.

'No, Kartik, I won't die, I promise you I won't die.'

That wasn't just a vague, soothing sound, meant to reassure a child. I meant it. I won't die if I can help it. It was when I was struggling to breathe that I knew what I was doing – I was working hard at not dying. Each breath I struggled to take was an affirmation of my will to live. I can't get away from that. After Baiajji died I badly wanted to know what it felt like to be dead. I used to lie flat on my back, my arms straight by my sides thinking, 'I'm dead like Baiajji, I can't feel anything, I won't feel anything'. For a while I used to feel myself suspended in nothingness. Then feeling would flow back, I would feel life tingling through me. I was alive, I could not be dead, I would never know what it felt like to be dead.

We're connected to our physical selves by the fragile thread of our wills. It's only when the thread snaps that it's all over. That hasn't happened to me, not as yet. I want to live. And I won't break down, I'm in full control of myself.

But those two days after Anu's death? I've told no one about this, not even Vanaa – I've lost those two days completely. I can remember nothing, there are only disjointed fragments. Flowers scattered on the grass. Two women talking, one of them leaning forwards, her face earnest. The woman's mouth moves, but there are no words, as if sound has been blocked out. People sitting in a huddle on a carpet; sunlight lighting up the fine hairs on a woman's face, giving her a lit-up look. And there is nothing to hold these disjointed bits together, not even the I-consciousness. This emptiness, this blankness frightens me.

When a child dies, there's so little left. After you've tidied and put away the clothes and the toys, there's nothing. Only emptiness. I feel I've emerged as the final victor in that game we used to play round the disused well in Ranidurg. All of us squatting round it, peering into its murky depths, trying to describe the horrors we said we

20

could see in there. The point was to say the most horror-rousing thing:

'I can see long white soft wriggly worms . . .'

'I can see green frothing bubbling scum – something is coming out of it – I can see one eye . . .'

The truth was that we could see nothing. There was just darkness. And a smell, the smell that was the worst thing about it, the smell we never spoke of because we could never find words for it. Now I know what it was. It was the smell of hopelessness. That's what haunts me now, the smell of hopelessness. I've lost hope entirely; I used it all up in that one day and night of frenzied hoping and there's nothing left. But hope is a fragile support anyway on which to rest the whole of your life. I can do without it. I will have to do without it. I have to live with the knowledge that it's real, that Anu's gone, that she will never return. It's cruel to leave the dead behind and go on, but we have no choice, we have to let them go.

Let them go? But it's Anu who won't let me go. She comes to me, over and over again she comes to me. I have hallucinations. I wake up to hear the soft snuffling sounds of her breathing by my side; I can smell her sweet baby flesh. Sometimes, as if I have gone back in time, her milky, ammoniac, talcum odour comes back to me; my breasts feel heavy and painful, as if they are gorged with milk. Once again I can feel the softness of her body in my arms, the heaviness of her head flopping over my shoulder; I can feel her toes, scrabbling at my midriff.

And there are memories. Strange that the memory that haunts me most often is that of her angry face when I tried to wean her. How resolutely she refused the bottle, how angrily she glared at me . . . No, I must reject these memories, I have to conquer them. This is one battle I have to win if I am to go on living. And yet my victory will carry with it the taint of betrayal. To forget is to betray.

But to go on like this is to wrong the living – Kartik above all, Kartik who watches me so anxiously, so fearfully. I cannot wrong him. I must let Anu go.

Why do I say that? She is gone. She just went, she never opened her eyes, never looked at me. Sometimes I think I could have borne it better if she had done that. To go without a word . . . ? But they all do that – Baiajji, Aju, and now Anu.

Amrut comes and stands by me, hesitant, as if wondering how to begin. I give him a few moments, then push away the books I'm sorting and speak to him myself. 'Go on, say it, why don't you? Are you scared?'

'Damn it, Didi, I am scared of you. People seeing us together always think I'm the tough guy and you're my delicate sister; they little know it's the other way round.'

'I'll say it for you then. You're going back to Delhi.'

'What a terrible thing it is to be so transparent. But that's the way I am – clear as day.'

'Have you told Inni you're going?'

'No, I thought I'd check with you first. Is it all right? I mean, are you okay?'

'Isn't there any other question you can ask me?'

'Well, you were ill.'

'I wasn't ill, it was just an attack of asthma.'

'Okay, okay, I grant it to you, you weren't ill. Prickly, aren't you?'

'Sit down here and listen to me, Ambu. I'm trying to get back to normal. I know nothing can undo what's happened, nothing can bring Anu back to me. And I know I have to go back to living. Why do I say "go back"? I *am* living.'

'I know, but . . .'

'Just give me time, for God's sake, give me some time. I can't bear people looking at me as if I'm – something abnormal. As if grief has pitted my skin or something. And

22

the platitudes I have to listen to! God, it's sickening! Someone gave me a Reader's Digest kind of comfort the other day, "Anyway, you've had her for a whole year. You should thank God for that." I won't. It isn't enough for me. I wanted her for my whole lifetime, I wanted a full life for her. I can see people thinking, "It was only a baby after all, does it matter so much?" Does a person's value increase with age? And up to what point? I can still remember someone saying after Aju died, "Well, he was old."'

'You have to put up with all this, Didi. Most of us are incapable of dealing with something as big as death, and so we talk nonsense.'

'Keep quiet, then. I'm not asking anyone for consolation, am I? I'm trying to deal with my grief myself. I don't need anyone.'

'Well, in a while, people will stop speaking of it to you.'

'And thank God for that! And you . . .'

'Hey, don't start on me now, what have I done?'

'All of you. I simply can't bear people tiptoeing about me as if I'm an invalid.'

'Okay, okay, we'll wear our shoes and stamp about the house. At least I will. That suit you better?'

'Oh, you silly clown, Ambu . . . I'm sorry I'm so sharp . . .'

'That's quite all right. I can imagine what it's like. And we're used to you . . .'

'Thanks. When are you leaving?'

'Friday. Is that all right?'

'It's your convenience you have to think of.'

'That suits me. It gives me the weekend to settle down. But, of course, I'm going only if you . . .'

'I am perfectly all right. How many times do I have to say it?'

'I say, don't pounce on me like that. I'm a nervous kind of fellow. Feel my heart beating . . . see that? Listen, Didi,

23

what I really want to say is, don't do this sort of thing again, will you?' He touches my forehead, like Harish had done.

'You think it was hysteria, don't you? It wasn't. It was a very deliberated action.'

'Why did you do it?' Amrut's face, entirely serious, as it so rarely is, tells me he really wants to know.

'Do you remember Baiajji's decoctions? No, of course, you won't, you were too little. She used to make the stuff for anyone convalescing. Remember what a disgustingly healthy kid I was? It's only for sick people, she used to tell me when I asked for it, and so I never got to drink it. But once I had fever for nearly a week, they thought it was typhoid. It wasn't and I recovered, but I had no appetite at all. Everything tasted like – what? Sawdust? No, like drainwater.'

'Yech, Didi, your similes!'

'And then Baiajji made me her decoction. I don't know what she put into it – pepper, I'm sure, and tamarind water, and oh, lots of things. You were supposed to sip it, but I was so eager to taste it, I gulped it down. And then – God, it was terrible. Hot and fiery, pungent and sour – no, I can't describe it. You have to taste it to know. Well, anyway, as soon as I drank it my nose began to run, my eyes began to water, my throat burnt – but you know what? I could taste. It was like a miracle. I could get the taste of everything after that.'

'And so?' Amrut asks, after waiting for me to go on.

'And so I banged my head against the wall. To feel something. Pain. Anything.'

'Hmm. Complex female, aren't you? Inni was telling me . . .'

'Yes? Go on.'

'Nothing.'

'Coward.'

'How right you are! Right, tell me then, what happened between you two in the morning?'

'Don't say "you two" in that superior manner – arbitrating between two silly quarrelsome females.'

'Well, what happened between you two superior beings – if an inferior male may ask?'

'Oh God, Amrut, I've forgotten how to laugh – it's almost painful. Isn't it terrible? As for what happened, well I woke up early – I always do these days – and I couldn't get back to sleep. I thought I'd make myself a cup of tea. I didn't want Inni to hear me, so I tiptoed past her room. But she heard me all the same and rushed out. She tried to make me go back to bed. She said she'd make the tea and bring it to me. She went on and on, as if I was an invalid, risking my life by getting out of bed. I kept telling her I was absolutely fine, I was amazingly patient. And you know, Ambu, I even smiled at her, pleasantly, to reassure her, you know . . .'

I must have unconsciously shaped my face into a smile, because Amrut exclaims, 'Like that? Gosh, no wonder she seemed terrified when I came out. Enough to unnerve anyone, let alone a sensitive plant like our poor Inni, to have her child grin at her that way at five in the morning.'

'Bereaved child – don't forget the important word. And so she wants to fuss over me. Even apart from the fact that I hate being fussed over, don't you see how unnatural it is, Ambu, to have her fussing over me? It's like a reversal of roles. When has she ever acted the doting mother with me . . . ?'

'She is your mother, Urmi.'

'Yes, but she never was the solicitous mother, was she? Even when all of you came to Ranidurg, it was I who looked after you. I prefer it that way.'

'Bossy female. Try to see her point of view, Didi . . .'

25

'And she should try to see mine. But I suppose it's hard for both of us to do that.'

'Just be patient, that's all. And gentle.'

'Why, Amrut, you've begun protecting Inni against me! Have you ever seen me being brutal to her? And why are you so forbearing with me? Can't you treat me normally?'

'This is normal. I've never stood up to you, don't expect me to begin now. It's too late for me to shake off the big-sister influence.'

'Do you put on this helpless-male act with your Dilliwali, Amrut?'

'What Dilliwali?' He's really offended. 'Can't you say her name?'

'Sorry Amrut, I meant Radha. We've got into the habit, I keep forgetting . . .'

'Sometimes I think you carry it too far, Vanaa and you . . .' he mumbles.

'I said I'm sorry. Stop grumbling. And look, you can go with an easy mind. I won't terrorise Inni, I promise you. I'll be gentle with her – soft as Kanchi silk.' I smile at him. 'Truly.'

'And you . . . ?'

'I'll be all right, I promise you that too.'

'What are you planning to do?'

'Go back to work, what else?'

'Are you sure, Didi? You want to go on with teaching?'

'What do you mean? I always wanted to teach.'

'I know. Gives you a chance to be bossy, huh?'

'I enjoy my classes.'

'Good enough for now, but I can't see you going on and on with undergraduate teaching. You've got to start on your doctorate work – last time you told me you'd start as soon as . . .'

'Anu was older, yes, I'd planned that.'

'Then get going, Didi, don't postpone it.'

'Do you know, Ambu, you sound like Papa. He always felt teaching was something too lowly for his daughter.'

'Papa! Don't compare me to him. I can never reach his heights of scathing sarcasm. And the way he looked at me – God, it really crushed me. It was a "I don't know what's going to happen to this useless fellow" look.'

'Poor Papa.'

'There was a time when you'd have said "poor Amrut". But it's no use expecting sympathy from you now that you're a parent. God, Didi, I'm sorry.'

'It's okay, Amrut. You think if you don't say these things, I don't remember Anu? There's nothing that doesn't remind me of her.'

'Didi, don't . . . I know how it is . . . please, Urmi, don't cry . . . please . . .'

He's patting my back, frantic little pats, as if that will some-how comfort me. His face, looking into mine, is terribly earnest. 'The pain will get less eventually – look at Inni . . .'

Suddenly I think of Inni sitting up, her face pinched, her voice hollow, going on and on, the night after Papa's funeral. She wouldn't rest, wouldn't sleep, she talked to us – to us? No, she was scarcely aware of us – the whole night through, of Papa, of how they met, of their courtship, their marriage, of things he said to her, endearments, intimacies. And all the while we sat by her, helpless, unable to stop her. Finally, when she was totally exhausted, Harish persuaded her to take a Calmpose and go to bed. And only then, when she fell asleep, did the whole burden of my own grief come upon me. A burden that seemed impossible to bear. And now . . . ? Papa is only a memory, a gentle memory.

'Never,' I say to Amrut fiercely, 'I will never stop suffering for Anu.'

I see a look of impatience on Amrut's face, mirroring, perhaps, the impatience I'd felt that night with Inni.

*

The monsoon announces itself with a melodramatic clap of thunder. Then, as if the day has decided to wind itself back into the night, it becomes dark. In a moment, the downpour begins. It is an awesome performance. The sound of rain and thunder fill the room; nothing else can be heard. In a while, it becomes part of the day, an accustomed sound, and the cries of the children as they run from windows to the balcony pierce through. It even becomes possible to talk at normal pitch.

'God, how I hate these Bombay rains! They frighten me. Remember the rains in Ranidurg? That was lovely. Grey skies, soft clouds, and a soothing drip drip.'

'Maddening drip drip, you mean. I prefer this. I remember your Ranidurg rains – everything damp and squelchy all the time . . .'

'It's damp and squelchy here too, Inniauntie.'

'And the slush – all that terrible red mud. I could never get the stains out of my petticoat hems. But the worst were those crawly things . . .'

'Why, Inniauntie, what a city person you are! What crawly things?'

'Those things that curl up into rings.'

'Oh, you mean the centipedes. Or, are they millipedes? Remember, Urmi, someone once told us that if we left them overnight in a box, they'd become silver rupee coins in the morning?'

'And did you?'

'Of course. What do you mean? A whole rupee – we'd do anything for that. The next morning mine was mercifully dead. But Urmi's had sort of oozed out some slimy stuff – the box was full of it.'

'Ugh, Vanaa, that's enough.'

We are, all of us, groping our way towards normality – whatever that normality is after a death in the family. But the effort is obvious – the sideways furtive glances at me,

28

the sudden flurry of talk at the threat of a silence. Vanaa and Inni are like two actors, desperately keeping the show going. They try, without seeming too obvious, to include me in their conversation; but it swells and eddies about me, leaving me untouched.

Only the children are free of any taint of artifice. They behave with me and in my presence as they have always done. Kartik keeps coming back to me though, as if for some kind of reassurance. It's an effort not to keep him close to me, not to cuddle him each time he sits by me. I resist the temptation and he wanders away.

The novelty of the rain wears off. Pallavi and Kartik go back to some game of theirs. Mandira, bored, becomes restless and fidgety.

'Mandira, don't switch on the light. It's so nice and cosy in the dark.'

'But, mummy, I want to read.'

'Mandira, don't, it's so nice in the dark.'

'You shut up, Pallavi. Mummy's little *chamchi*.' She repeats in a mocking tone 'It's so nice in the dark!'

'Mummy, she's saying bad words.'

'*Chamchi* isn't a bad word.'

'What does it mean?'

'Who cares? Urmiauntie, shall I comb your hair?'

'If you want to.'

'Don't let her, Urmi, you know she'll get it all tangled and knotted,' Vanaa warns me, speaking in Kannada.

'It's all right. Ouch, Mandira, go slow, child.'

'I told you so!'

'I haven't even begun, I'm just opening your plait and you're making such a fuss, Urmiauntie. Don't move, I'll go and get your comb.' She runs into my room and is out in a moment. 'Is this your comb? Okay, sit quiet.'

'Mandira, for God's sake, stop torturing her.'

29

'I'm not torturing, I'm doing a hair-style. And Urmiauntie lets me do it. Why do you come in the middle?'

'In the middle! The language these children speak! Why don't we speak our own language?'

'Which one is that?'

'That's quite a question you've asked, Inniauntie!'

'I can speak four,' Mandira announces. 'English, Marathi, Gujerati, Hindi . . .'

'You sound like Urmi's Baiajji. She was so proud of her Hindi, poor thing. It was the oddest Hindi, I couldn't understand a word of it.'

'Five,' Mandira calls out. 'I can speak five. I forgot Kannada.'

'Kannada! Ha!'

'You think when you talk to Urmiauntie in Kannada I can't understand, but I can understand everything. I know what you said to her just now when I wanted to comb her hair . . .'

'Five languages. And looks like you're going to end up a hairdresser!'

'If she does, Vanaa, what do you think your mother will say?'

'Akka? God knows. I just can't imagine. I can still remember all the things she said to me when I told her I was sick of school and studying and all I wanted was to get married, stay at home, look after my husband and children . . .'

'There, Urmiauntie, I've finished. Do you want to see? Shall I get you a mirror? Wait, I'll get it. See, isn't it nice? Urmiauntie, you look beautiful.'

'Look beautiful, do I?'

'Don't make faces like that, you're spoiling everything.'

'Thank you, Mandira, for saying such a nice thing to me.'

'Why are you laughing, mummy? You're laughing at me.'

'She's not laughing at you, she's laughing at the idea of me being beautiful.'

'No, she's laughing at me. You're always making fun of me. You're cruel. I'll never talk to you again, never, never in my life . . .'

'Mandira . . .'

'Leave her alone, Inniauntie. If you grovel before her, it takes her that much longer to get off her high horse.'

But Inni walks out after Mandira and conversation dries up. Vanaa drops her 'being normal' act; she looks apprehensively at me and suddenly, to break the silence, asks, 'Shall I plait your hair for you, Urmi?'

'No, it's okay,' I say, twisting it into a knot.

'Vanaatai . . .' Rekha's voice comes to us, 'the picture is beginning. Don't you want to come and watch?'

'Shall we?' Vanaa looks at me doubtfully.

'Of course.' Vanaa still seems hesitant. I know she is thinking of the last time we did this. When was that? Time unrolls itself – before Kishore came home, before we went out on our holiday, before . . .

'What else can we do when it's raining? It'll keep the children quiet for a while, anyway. Come on.'

I walk out briskly and Vanaa follows me. It is a relief, anyway, to sit and watch, not to talk, to let the meaningless sounds fill the room. I have a sudden understanding of Rekha's fascination with this movie world, so far from her own slum home, from her life as a drudge in people's homes. She is already rapt, though it's only the commercials as yet; when the movie begins, she will be wholly lost, ready to give it the response it demands. Vanaa and I settle down and we are all of us grouped about the TV as usual – Inni elegantly dressed, as if prepared to go out, Rekha, on the floor by her, Vanaa sprawling comfortably, the two younger children about her. Mandira, always slightly aloof,

31

is even more so today after the spat with her mother. Only I . . .

The commercials are over and the credits for the movie have just ended when Priti walks in. She does not enter at once. Shedding her slippers near the door, she stands there for a moment, taking in the scene. 'How cosy!' she exclaims.

Vanaa, as if her percipience is sharpened by Priti's presence and words, looks round, laughs and says, 'Squalid, you mean. Paper and plastic bags – such ugly litter, isn't it? Come in, Priti and join the pig-sty.'

Vanaa and I had once argued about this attitude of Priti's. 'It's a pose, that's what it is,' Vanaa had said 'all this talk of her love of togetherness and family warmth and closeness. It's phoney. She thinks she has to say these things. But she doesn't really need them; she just likes to think of herself as wistfully longing for them.'

'I don't agree. I don't think it's a pose. It's genuine. Think of that lonely childhood of hers . . .'

'I've heard plenty about it. The sad little only child . . .'

'Don't forget, Vanaa, she was in a foreign country, with both her parents working. That would make anyone nostalgic about these things.'

'Theoretically, perhaps. But I don't think people can really get away from their beginnings. I mean, the kind of life you've lived as a child, it's always the norm for you, whether you like it or not. Look at your own Baiajji – remember how she created an atmosphere of rural life around herself? All those cattle she kept and the manure lying around. You know, Urmi, I can still remember you saying to Inniauntie, when she turned up her nose at the cattle shed, "It's not the dung that stinks, Inni, it's the urine."'

'I said that? Gosh, I can imagine Inni's reaction to that!'

'But about Priti – the truth is that she flourishes in isolation.'

32

'The truth is that you don't like her very much and you're just being bitchy – or catty – about her.'

Perhaps I've imbibed something of Vanaa's critical faculties which makes me notice now how gracefully Priti gets into the scene. Part of her training as an actress, perhaps. She lingers by Inni, almost paying court to her.

'Amrut's gone?'

'Yes, he left on Friday. We haven't seen you for quite a while, Priti.'

'I was out of town, I'd gone to see my father. Hello, Vanaa . . .'

She greets the three children by their names before she turns to me. For the first time, she falters. She has come to condole with me, but something stops her from saying what she's prepared to say; perhaps she feels me holding her sympathy at bay. In her confusion she blunders. 'Back to normal?' she asks.

As soon as she asks the question, she realises her mistake. Vanaa helps her out by rushing in with, 'Shall I turn off this blessed thing? You've given us a good excuse to do it.'

'That's okay, Vanaa, I'll sit and watch too. I can't remember how long it's been since I saw one of those old movies. Which one is it today?'

Everyone looks blank. Vanaa laughs.

'Well, never mind, just tell mc what's happened till now.'

'Oh, all kinds of original things – like the hero and heroine started off by being hostile, now they've just discovered they're in love, the heroine is a poor village girl and the hero is a rich city man . . .'

'Mummy, please!'

'Okay, Mandira, I shall be dumb. You'll have to make sense of it on your own, I'm afraid, Priti. I can't help you any more.'

'I'll try my best.'

We settle down as the hero, flinging his hair off his forehead, turns a quizzical look on the heroine and bursts into song, praising her beauty. She listens, coy, complacent, little-girlish.

'I don't know how you can watch this rubbish,' Papa had said despairingly to Amrut and me once. I had tried to explain: the thing is to enter into it wholeheartedly, to enjoy all its improbabilities and foolishness. A small touch of criticism and the charm is lost. But Papa could never understand. He would have looked down with even greater scorn if he had known about what Amrut and I did occasionally – acting out the scenes, parodying the dialogues, the situations, exaggerating everything so that it became bizarre. Vanaa had been our appreciative audience in those days. But Vanaa was, she confesses even now, dazzled by us.

'I fell in love with your whole family. I thought Inniauntie was the most beautiful woman in the world and your father the most dignified, and yes, the richest . . . It was because of those cars standing before your house whenever he came. And Amrut and you dazzled me. You were so different from all the children I'd known till then.'

The movie meanders on. The lovers' idyll is rudely disturbed by the villain who desires the heroine as well. He tries to take advantage of her when she is alone, but the hero comes there just in time. The screen explodes into sudden violence. Fists, muscles, grunts; macho images fill the room. The battered villain swears revenge. He soon gets his opportunity. The heroine, decoyed by a message she thinks is from the hero, is all alone with the villain in a ruined temple. He stands, arms akimbo, staring at the girl, a lustful smile on his face. The girl's anger dissolves into terror. A quality of uneasiness fills the room. Suddenly I wonder, should we let the children watch this? Vanaa gets the same thought. 'Shall we switch it off?'

34

'No, mummy, please don't.'

'Don't worry, they'll have done all the censoring necessary.'

The villain's back fills the screen, then the girl's anguished face as she backs away from him, arms held out before her, defensively, appealingly. The back moves, muscles ripple across its expanse, the girl's mouth opens in a scream . . .

'Cut.'

'Thank God! The censors never fail us, do they?'

'What happened, mummy? What did he do?'

'He hit her.'

Priti laughs. Vanaa makes a face at her. 'You're telling lies,' Mandira charges her. 'I know what happened.'

'Keep it to yourself,' Vanaa says wryly.

The commercials come on. It's time for the news. I get up and in spite of Inni's protest make us a cup of tea, strong, sweet, milky *desi* tea, as Vanaa demands. The movie resumes and, just as Harish joins us, reaches its tear-sogged end – the villain dead, the hero nobly offering to marry the heroine despite her 'spoiled' state, the heroine just as nobly refusing and then dying at his feet, her purity restored by his forgiveness.

'Well, all over?'

We come slowly out of our torpor, even the children move like zombies. I switch off the TV and there is a sudden flurry of activity. Rekha whisks about the room, collecting the plates and cups. She dumps them into the sink and shouts a cheerful 'ta-ta' to everyone before leaving, banging the door as she goes. Inni, who can never get used to this kind of free and easy behaviour in servants, closes her eyes. Harish, full of his usual Sunday bonhomie, is ready to take the women and children out for a treat. He is masterful. 'Never mind the time,' he says, hustling us into getting ready. I'm the only one who stays out of the bustle.

'Urmi, aren't you coming?'

'No, Harish, if you don't mind . . .'

Inni suddenly balks at leaving me alone. 'Inni, I'm not an invalid,' I argue with her. But she is adamant. It's only when Priti says, 'I'll be around, Inniauntie, for some more time,' that Inni gives in. 'Don't do the washing up', she warns me as they leave. But the moment the door closes behind her, I make for the kitchen.

'I thought you weren't supposed to . . .' Priti follows me.

'Oh, that's Inni's usual fuss. You know how Monday mornings are. Rekha sulks when she sees all this piled up. Anyway, I find these chores relaxing.'

'Do you? Frankly, I find them a pain.'

'You're lucky you came back to India.'

'I know. I thank God every day I can leave this drudgery to someone else. Here, let me dry. Can I use this? No, really, I'll feel more comfortable if I help.'

I can see Priti nerving herself to speak; finally she says it. 'You don't mind, do you Urmi, if I say that I know how you feel about Anu?'

I am silent. She gives me a look and goes on. 'I haven't told anyone about this, but I had an ectopic pregnancy. I can't have a child – ever. So you see, I can imagine, a little bit, what it is like . . .'

I put my hand briefly on hers. Then it's over and behind us. I feel I've gained a victory. I've been able to face her sympathy. As we work – Priti, unused to such work, is slow and clumsy and the washed cups and plates pile up before her – we talk of the movie we've just watched. Priti is indignant. 'They're harmful,' she says, 'so divorced from reality.'

'Who wants reality?' I ask her. 'At one time our grandmothers told us fairy tales, now we have these. They're much more exciting than real life, aren't they? Look at the marriage thing. You know how it is in real life – absolutely

36

cold-blooded. I've seen people weighing up the families, their social status, money. And the couple too – height, weight, education – God! In the movies, it's a total lack of parity.'

'I know.' And Priti chants, 'Rich man/poor girl, simple man/sophisticated girl, city man/village girl . . .'

'That's a hoary tradition, it began with Kalidasa.'

'Kalidasa!' She looks at me puzzled, unsure of my attitude. Am I serious? Finally she laughs.

'I'm serious. Tell me, what's Shakuntala but a simple village girl? And Dushyanta? He's the classical city roue.'

'I never thought of that. But, Urmi, don't these movies make you angry? They're such total male fantasies . . .'

'Well, what do you expect? They're made by men and so . . .'

'I know. That's why . . .'

In the silence that falls between us, I can sense the ghost of Mira.

'Why did you tell her about Mira?' Vanaa had asked me, the day she had realised, from something Priti said, that she knew about Mira.

'Why shouldn't I have?' I had countered defensively.

But I had been angry with myself, nevertheless. Why had I spoken to her of Mira? I hadn't intended to. I was led into it, carried away by an argument with Priti, using Mira's story finally to prove my point. We were arguing about a judgement in a case filed by a husband against his wife for restitution of conjugal rights. Priti was excited that the judge had ruled that the wife could not be forced into a sexual relationship with the husband against her will.

'Isn't it radical, absolutely earth-shaking, in this country, I mean? Can you imagine the consequences?'

'What consequences?' I asked her. 'One judgement by a single judge – which can be appealed against and over-ruled . . .'

'It's a precedent,' she said.

'If women can afford to go to court,' I corrected her. 'How many women do you see going to court on such a matter?'

'This woman did.'

Priti refused to see how special the case was. The wife, after the couple parted, had entered films and was making a name for herself; at which point the husband decided he wanted her back. 'The woman is an actress – she's capable of earning a hell of a lot of money. Naturally her family would like to see her free of her husband so that he won't get any control over that money. That's why they're backing her. Otherwise they'd have said, like all parents do, "Go back to your husband like a good girl."'

'This is a beginning,' Priti insisted. 'Once you know the law can help you – if one woman can win the right to her own body . . .'

'It's never enough. It's like saying, "Look, we have a woman Prime Minister; look how much our women have progressed; look how free they are." One Indira Gandhi in charge of the nation and a country full of women not allowed to take charge of their own lives . . . No, Priti, laws can't change people's lives.'

'Oh, you're hopeless,' Priti said in exasperation, 'you're a cynic, a pessimist . . .'

'I'm a realist. Nothing will change.'

It was then that I said, 'There will always be Miras.' And the very next day she came to me and said, 'I have an idea. It came to me in a flash last night. Let's make a movie on Mira, let's recreate her life.'

I can remember that morning so clearly, when we spoke of Mira, Priti and I, the two of us sitting at the kitchen table, doused in kitchen smells and sounds, the clutter of breakfast things between us. And Anu, restless as always, trying to clamber up, using my legs as a ladder, slipping down over and over again, but determinedly going on, until Shanta came and took her away. Meanwhile, Priti, intent on what she had come to say, went on talking. 'Something went click inside me last night when you spoke of Mira. I had a queer feeling I've heard this story before, I know this woman, I know her story. This,' she said with such emphasis that the word came hissing between her teeth, 'this is what I've been waiting for all these years, this is the movie I'm going to make, this is the story I'm going to tell.'

Priti has a penchant for dramatic phrases. I'm used to her; most of them mean nothing. Yet I felt an uneasiness as she said this, a sense of something wrong, something jarring. Then I remembered I'd felt the same uneasiness when, recalling her decision to return to India all by herself, she'd spoken of her 'moment of truth'.

'It was Robert Kennedy's death,' she said. 'I saw him lying spread-eagled in that narrow corridor and I knew at that moment that I could no longer stay in a country that could suffer such pointless violence. I knew then I had to come home. It was my moment of truth,' she had ended, linking her sixteen-year-old self to a Gandhi or a Buddha.

Unaware of my reaction to her excitement, Priti continued. 'I've always known I wouldn't go on making ad films with Avinash, I knew I'd go on to my own work some day. It was just that I had to wait for the right time, the right idea. And now I have it . . .' She tried to draw me into the vortex of her own excitement. 'It'll be beautiful, I can feel it in my bones. I'll make it soft, muted, nothing garish or loud. And give it a feeling of the period – just before Independence, wasn't it? And you say you have her poems? We'll use them, set them to music; perhaps I can use one throughout as a kind of theme song . . .' She went on and on, her bangles clinking, her breasts jiggling, a hundred words where ten would do, a hundred gestures where one would suffice.

'I want you to give me the story,' she said finally, and

39

waited for my answer, which was an instant, instinctive 'No!' She was taken aback, but recovered in a moment. 'Right then, give me the papers and I'll . . .'

She saw the involuntary clutching movement of my hands. 'If you'd rather not, then write it for me yourself, any way you want . . . Why, that's a wonderful idea, Urmi. Yes, Urmi you do the script for me. It still haunts me, the way you told me about it last night. I want your vision, Urmi, a woman's vision.' It was the first time she said that phrase.

She brushed aside all my objections. Starting on my doctorate work? Pooh! Who wanted another thesis on James Joyce, R. K. Narayan or whoever? My job? Oh, I could take leave, couldn't I? And if there were problems, she'd pay me, yes, she would, as much as my job did. The children? Kartik was already in full-day school, wasn't he? And Anu? I had Shanta, to look after her, didn't I? And Inni was at home as well. What was my problem, for heaven's sake?

Finally I said, 'But Priti, she's Kishore's mother.'

And she said, 'Do you have to get bogged down in the personal? Don't you understand, she's not just herself, she's a symbol. We need symbols to focus attention on the things the symbols stand for . . .'

She's not a symbol, she's Mira who wrote *This book is mine as all can tell, if you steal it you will go to hell*, the girl who wrote '*Strictly private and confidential*' on her books.

'Would you use your own mother's life?' I asked Priti.

And she said, 'Yes. One has got to be objective; one has to distance oneself.'

And then she went on to the line of how we had to know our mothers and grandmothers to know our situations. And now, I thought, she will quote Virginia Woolf to me. She did. And I knew then I could not work with her. I never could. I said so to her, but I didn't tell her my real reason –

40

that I could not trust the integrity of a person who could so glibly speak of the need to know our mothers and grand-mothers, yet so successfully block her own mother out of her life. For the truth was that Priti, in speaking of her decision to return to India, had left her mother out of it entirely. It was Vanaa who had told me about Priti's mother. She had, on one of her annual visits to India, run over a number of people sleeping on the pavement, since which time she'd become a manic depressive. An alcoholic as well, she had made life at home impossible for her ado-lescent daughter so that Priti had had to get out. I could understand, I could sympathise with Priti's need to blank this out, but not the dishonesty that alchemised the truth, making, in the process, a heroine of herself, linking a personal decision to a moment of national drama.

She argued with me, but I said nothing. Perhaps, because of my silence she thought she would be able to impose her will on mine. 'I know,' she said as she left me, 'we will do this together. I know you'll work with me on Mira's story.'

How glibly she said 'Mira', how easily I say the name now. For years I had not even known that her name was Mira. She was Kishore's mother who died when he was born. It was Akka who gave her her name that day. 'This is Mira,' she said, pointing to a face in a photograph.

And it is Akka I see when I think of that evening, Akka saying 'This is Mira', Akka reading the poems to us, Akka crying . . .

Happiness, after a time of sorrow, seems like another country, distant and unreal. That is how I see it now, a picture of us on that evening – Akka, her bad leg stretched out before her, trying one key after another on the ancient lock of the trunk, Vanaa, the girls, Kartik and I watching, breathless. And the sigh, the sound that came from us when finally a key fitted and there was a click. The smell that sprang out at us when the lid creaked open; a smell difficult to connect with the oblong piece of sandalwood that lay right on top. Sealed in for too long, the fragrance had been lost; it had become just a smell, neither pleasant nor unpleasant, merely distinctive.

And then we saw the books. The weight of the trunk should have prepared us for them, but we were surprised when Akka brought them out. A variety of books. Textbooks, with a student's comments scribbled all over. Notebooks of an earlier era, the cardboard covers severely simple. A few novels, both in Kannada and English, looking used and much-read. Untidy bundles of paper, scraps really, torn from notebooks. Scribbling pads, old diaries scribbled all over, not a page left blank. Then a file. And, finally, at the bottom of the trunk, an envelope. Photographs cascaded out of it, the moment Akka picked it up, and lay scattered before us. Akka lifted one, looked at it, put her finger on a face and said, 'This is Mira'.

'Mira? Mira who?'

'Kishore's mother. Kartik's grandmother.'

While the children questioned and exclaimed, and Vanaa and Akka explained to them that Akka was not really Kishore's mother, only Vanaa's, I picked up the photograph. I have it here with me. It is a studio photograph of a group of girls – Mira and her friends – formally posed by the photographer against the classical backdrop of a black curtain. The faces, even after the years, stand out sharp and clear against the dark background. Three girls are sitting on chairs, three of them stand at the back. Mira is standing ramrod stiff, arms by her sides, her longish face solemn. Her hair is parted right in the centre – a clean straight line shows on her scalp – and her two plaits have been doubled and secured with ribbons on either side of her face. She is wearing a blouse with long sleeves and a V-

42

neck, the sari stiffly arranged on the shoulder so as to display the border. From the formality of the picture I imagine it was taken to mark an occasion – Mira's wedding perhaps – a parting of ways for a group of friends, the end of a chapter. Is that the reason for Mira's rather melancholy look? I struggled then, I try again, to see a resemblance to Kishore; but it is impossible. She remains a girl belonging to a certain period – her clothes, the way she has done her hair, fixing her into it, like a fly in amber. And yet, are the eyes, guarded, unwilling to reveal anything, Kishore's? But perhaps that is just a result of the solemnity of the occasion; she is being photographed and is therefore offering herself to the camera as a subject.

It was with the books that Mira suddenly came alive. 'Look at this,' Vanaa said to me, showing me a copy of *The Golden Treasury*. A dog-eared, much-thumbed copy. 'Read this,' Vanaa said, pointing to the flyleaf: 'To Mira on her 13th birthday from her loving father.' And below that, in a different hand: *This book is mine as all can tell, if you steal it you will go to hell*.

I laughed but Vanaa, infinite pity in her voice, said, 'Oh, the poor thing.' I felt no pity. There was only a throb of excitement. As if in opening the book, we had released a genie; she came alive, she was suddenly all about us – in the books with her notes scribbled all over, in the scraps of paper on which she had written words, lines in Kannada. And there was a green and gold covered magazine – the annual journal of her college – which fell open at a page on which there was a long poem. I read out the name of the contributor: 'Mira Purohit Jr. B.A.'

'She wrote poetry,' Vanaa and I exclaimed simultaneously.

We tried to read out the poem in the journal, struggling with the script that had become unfamiliar through the

43

years. 'Let's ask Akka to read it out to us,' Vanaa said finally, impatiently snatching the journal out of my hands.

I remember how reluctantly Akka turned to us from the children – they were still looking at the photographs – listened to Vanaa, took the journal and read the poem to herself. 'Read it aloud, Akka,' Vanaa prodded her, but Akka ignored her until she had read all of it. I heard Anu cry, brought her out and fed her; in a while she went back to sleep. Akka began to read, slowly, in her school teacher's voice. '*The Road Builders*' she began solemnly.

It was less a poem, more a song to be chanted, and that is how Akka did it.

> *Come, my brothers, come, my sisters,*
> *let us join our hands;*
> *a new road, a new way*
> *a new age begins.*

The children loved the joyous lilt of the refrain, waited impatiently for it to come, and joined Akka in chanting '*On to work, hai-sa, all together, hai-sa.*' Anu's face, severe in sleep, broke up, her lips pouted as if she was going to cry. Suddenly the face relaxed, the lips moved, twitched, became a smile.

'There's another one of hers here. Shall I read it?'

'Yes, yes,' we clamoured.

And then the lights went out. The children screamed in delight, ran about the room, stumbling over one another, over us. I settled Anu on Vanaa's lap and went in to get a light. When I returned with the lantern, it swung, so that the light fell momentarily on Akka's face. She was leaning against the wall, her legs stretched out before her, in the habitual pose of women weary at the end of the day. Her face looked old – or was it just a trick of the shadows? I set the lantern by her and went back to my place. The children

44

returned to the circle of light, Pallavi immediately lying down, pillowing her head on her grandmother's lap. I can remember how the room looked – all movement – as the flickering light set the shadows on the wall dancing and quivering. We were silent and still now, even the children hypnotised into silence by our solemnity. Pallavi, soothed perhaps by her grandmother's stroking hand, fell asleep. Akka read this poem, a much longer poem, softly, as if conscious of the two sleeping children. This one was about a singer who went singing past her (Mira's?) house every morning, before daylight.

The eastern light lifts the veil of darkness,
the sparrow chirps on the swinging bough,
the calf cries for its mother in the barn,
the world stretches, opens its eyes.

When she came to the last verse, Akka was so soft she was almost inaudible.

Palanquin-borne, the notes rise and fall,
like motes in the sunshine they float in the air
now they come galloping, riding on a raaga
the last plaintive notes and he is gone.

Slowly, thoughtfully Akka put the magazine down. 'So she wrote poetry.'

Now it made sense. The scraps of paper scribbled over were the beginnings, the working out of her poems, the file with long ruled pages in it, one poem to a page, had all the completed ones. 'Let me see those,' Akka said. Vanaa gave her the file and she started to read. Vanaa and I, the two older children hampering us, were trying to clear up, to put things back into the trunk, when we heard a strange sound. We looked up to see Akka crying. Her face hidden in her

45

sari, she wept with such abandon that her body shook and heaved. There was something frightful about it, like a bout of incontinence in a normal, healthy person. Vanaa and Mandira both moved to Akka, and of the two it was Mandira who looked more adult. Vanaa, her lips trembling, her chin quivering like a child's on the brink of tears, could do nothing but repeat 'Akka'. It was Mandira who put her arms about her grandmother and said tenderly, 'Don't cry, Ajji.'

Akka stopped abruptly at that. Her body became still, her face emerged from her sari, wiped clean of both the tears and the emotion that had brought them on. At that moment the lights came on. Akka smiled at Mandira and said, 'Let's get dinner ready; come with me.' She moved Pallavi's head to my lap saying, 'Kartik, get me some curry leaves, child,' and went out with both the children. In a while, the smell of hot oil came to us, the sounds of mustard seeds spluttering, the curry leaves sizzling in oil. It was like a reassurance. Akka was all right again.

Vanaa sat up, her face lost its terrified-little-girl's look. She lifted the glass shade of the lantern, tilting it to blow it out. I can see her face, the powdery glint of dried tears on her cheeks, I can hear the jingle of her glass bangles as she put the lantern down. For a second, as the flame went out, the smell of kerosene lingered in the room. 'Come to eat,' Kartik sang out, and I gently eased Pallavi's head off my lap, so that I could carry Anu back to bed.

That night, before going to bed, Akka told us Mira's story. No, not her story, just the story of her marriage. Akka had been quiet that evening as she cooked and cleared up; it was not her usual quiet, more a kind of reflectiveness. We were already in bed by the time she finished her work for the day, all of us sleeping as usual in a row on the floor of the large hall. The children had fallen asleep, Vanaa was reading, and I was giving Anu her last night feed. Akka sat by me. When Anu fell asleep, she gently lifted her off my

46

lap and put her on the mattress, wiping the milk off her chin. (Oh God, this hurts, why do I have to think of this? But must I blot Anu from my memories to save myself pain?) She sat, staring at the sleeping child, while I got ready to lie down.

'Why aren't you sleeping, Akka?' Vanaa asked.

Without replying to that question, Akka told us the story of Mira's marriage. She spoke fluently, as if she had been shaping it in her mind all evening. To me the story – the way she told it to us – is not so much about Mira's marriage, but about the man's obsession with her. He saw her at a wedding and fell in love with her. After which he became a man in single-minded pursuit of an object: marrying Mira. It was not very easy. He could not propose directly to her, he knew his mother would never countenance such a marriage. Nor could he ask his parents to propose to her parents on his behalf – such a thing was not done. And so he went at it deviously; and it is this, more than anything else, that gives me a clue to his feelings, his tenacity. He induced a mutual friend to suggest his name to Mira's parents as a possible groom for their daughter. After this was done, they went through the whole complicated process of settling a marriage – he had to conceal his eagerness from his parents through it all – and they were married.

'How do you know all this?' Vanaa asked her mother.

'It was your aunt who told me this, she did it the day I entered this house. But she'd warned me even earlier, "My brother was crazy about his wife," she said. "I've never seen any man like that. And since her death," she said, "it's his son." He brought the day-old baby away with him the day after the funeral, she told me, nobody could stop him. What he really wants now is a mother for that motherless child.'

The cruelty, the enormous cruelty of that silenced us.

We said nothing. As if our silence was a reproof she said, 'I'm glad she was frank. I knew then what to expect.'

The same night she gave me the trunk. 'Take this, Urmi, it's Mira's.' She gave it to me with the same formality with which she had given me the little bits of Mira's jewellery. Only then she hadn't said 'Mira'. 'They're Kishore's mother's,' she had said, 'I kept them for his wife.' But this time she said, 'Take this, it's Mira's.' She did not mention Kishore at all, as if she was now directly linking me with Mira.

But it was not Mira I thought of when I looked at the trunk. She paled into insignificance before the woman who had so shocked us with her sudden bout of grief. Akka, who hadn't cried when her husband died, who had been stoical while Vanaa sobbed like a child when she went to Bombay to study, who had been calm even when Vanaa got married and went away – why had she broken down now?

I opened the trunk and began to read Mira's poems. When I came to a small poem about a newly married couple, I suddenly stopped. It began joyfully enough (*Oh, look at them, the women cried/with knowing looks and teasing eyes*), comparing them to the divine couple Laxmi-Narayan. Then, in the last stanza, the tone changed with a shocking abruptness. After I read it, I knew it was this poem that had moved Akka to tears. And I put the trunk away. But she comes back to me now, the sprightly girl who wrote *This book is mine as all can tell, if you steal it you will go to hell*, the woman who wrote those poems in the solitude of an unhappy marriage, who died giving birth to her son at twenty-two.

Inni and Kartik come home to find me scrabbling in the cupboards. 'What are you doing?' Inni asks. I explain. She looks blank, bored. But Kartik exclaims, 'The black trunk? I know, it's in the loft.' The excitement of the search gets to him. He joins me in dragging the tall stool from the

48

balcony, he clambers up, crawls into the loft. Inni is annoyed. 'What a time,' she keeps saying, yawning loudly every minute. My heart is in my mouth as Kartik disappears into the darkness of the loft. I shine a torch into its depths to help him. 'I got it, Mama,' he calls out, his voice emerging muffled. 'It's heavy.'

'Push it to the edge, Kartik.'

He comes out triumphant, festooned with cobwebs, the trunk before him. I take it down and send him, protesting, to have a bath. By the time he returns, his hair wet and slicked down, his face clean, blurred with sleep, I am ready for bed myself. Somehow I know now is not the time to do any more. I also know the next time I open the trunk, it will be in search of Mira.

'Urmi . . .'

'What is it, Inni?'

'What's three little words of prayer?'

It takes me a moment to realise she's doing the crossword. I have to think before I can reply, 'Orison.'

'What?'

'Or-is-on. That's prayer.'

'Yes, of course, I knew it, but . . .'

She will now consult the dictionary, look up the word and I can go back – to what? What am I doing? I've been working and have it all in order now. I've smoothed out the scraps of paper, put the notebooks in chronological order, piled the other books together and dusted the ancient file. It looks very businesslike; almost, the thought comes to me, as if this is the material for my dissertation. For a second I linger over the idea, then laugh at myself.

But what am I doing with these papers of Mira? Playing a game with myself? Was this what Aju was doing all those years when we were told, 'Sssh, don't make so much noise, Aju's working'? It was a kind of family legend that he was writing a history of his Raja's family. After his death, Papa and I searched for his papers, but there was nothing, not a page, not a scrap, not a word. I can remember Papa's face at the end of our search. He looked cheated, cheated of the legend of his father as a writer, perhaps. He tried desperately to revive it, 'Maybe he gave the manuscript to someone, maybe he burnt it, maybe it's still somewhere'; but it was no use. The legend was dead; Aju had been no writer. We never spoke of it again, Papa and I, as if to admit it was treachery.

Mira is different. The piles of paper, the books before me, prove that. She loved even the physical act of writing, I can see it in these pages of quotations from other writers she's lovingly copied out – pages and pages of them. Her handwriting is neat, the letters childishly rounded, each letter perfectly formed. But in this book of notes she took down in college, the writing is a careless scrawl. She has broken off at times to write some personal comments, and the different subjects often run into one another. But there is a workmanlike orderliness about her file of poems, one poem to a page, each carefully written out. None of the poems have titles, though. And there's something else – how is it I never noticed it until now? – the fascinating dichotomy in her writing. Her diaries, every word of them, are in English, the poems are in Kannada. But why do I call it a fascinating dichotomy? That's such a Priti-like thought. Don't we, all of us, slip from one language to another according to the need of the moment? (Except, it occurs to me, Baiajji, a real confused polyglot, who invariably spoke the wrong language, blissfully unaware that the person couldn't understand a word of what she was saying.) But here, in Mira's papers, the line is drawn with an absolute clarity – her thoughts in English, her creative writing in Kannada. It is certainly strange.

And who, I wonder now, put these papers together in

this trunk? Her mother was lucky, she died first, she never had to clear away her dead daughter's belongings. It was some of the women, I imagine, who disposed of her clothes and locked away Mira's jewels. And then her husband, yes, it has to be her husband, found these papers. I can see him collecting them, piling them in this trunk, locking it and putting it away. Did he read the papers? Perhaps, seeing these old notebooks, he thought they were relics of her college life and so he left them alone. Why did she keep these notebooks? A link with happier, lighthearted times? I think of her flipping over the pages, smiling at the girl who had written these things in her classroom.

For a moment I have a thought of showing these books to Kishore. He has never once spoken to me of his dead mother. Something tells me that if I show him these, if I speak of her, his face will take on what I call his 'closed room look'. It's like Mira's warning on the first page of all her diaries: *Strictly private and confidential*.

Why do I call them diaries? They're not elegant, leather-covered volumes, but tattered old notebooks, every little bit, even the margins, scribbled on. This is not a daily account of her routine life, but a communion with herself.

'Mira's story,' Priti said. Mira's story lies here. And I find myself hesitant to trespass, to violate her privacy, to lay bare her tragic story.

Tragic? It's hard to think of her as a tragic being when I see this picture of her. It's an outdoor one, taken, perhaps, at a picnic. Mira is sitting by a stream, her sari pulled up to her knees, showing her plump calves, dabbling her feet in water, one foot a little higher than the other, as if she was childishly kicking at the water when the person behind the camera said 'Smile'. And she did. An impish smile that animates her face, splits it into two. A smile extraordinarily like Kartik's rare one.

51

'Look,' I showed him, 'your grandmother. Doesn't she look a bit like you?'

'Like me?' He absorbed it gravely, then smiled, pleased. But Inni didn't agree. 'She's not a bit like Kartik,' she said crossly.

As a matter of fact, she's right. Kartik is a beautiful child and Mira was a plain one – obvious in this picture of a family group taken on the occasion of a brother's thread ceremony. The boy, with his shaven head and begging bowl, is sitting in the place of honour between his parents; Mira and the other brother have been posed by the photographer, with his professional sense of symmetry, behind the parents – the boy behind his mother, Mira behind her father. Mira, however, is standing a little away – something in her stance makes it seem deliberate – avoiding the camera, while the rest of them are looking obediently into it. She is frowning, her face sulky, her eyes squinting into the sun. Yes, a plain child.

And yet Priti would have made her beautiful. Perhaps she's right; a heroine has to have beauty. And the man? Perched beside Priti, on her feminist soapbox, I know what I'd have had to make of him: a brutal, insensitive man. Perhaps he was insensitive; but brutal?

I remember I always felt a little sorry for him; my last memories of him are of a pathetic, faded, ghost-like man in a wheel chair. Before that he had been a cheerful kind of man, hopefully offering us jokes that were hard to laugh at ('Going to play bad-minton or good-minton?' he asked Vanaa and me once, seeing us with rackets in our hands.) Vanaa, however, never failed to laugh at his jokes. She was a kind girl. Or was it sycophancy? Maybe she laughed so that he would notice her. But he never did. For him, there was only Kishore.

We grumbled once, Amrut and I, about Papa and his expectations of us. 'He expects too much of us,' Amrut complained. 'We've got to come up to his standards of achievement, and that's expecting too much – at least of me.'

'Well, I'm lucky,' Vanaa said matter-of-factly, 'my father expects nothing from me. In fact, I wonder whether he knows I exist.'

She said it unemotionally, but her face made me long to comfort her. Maybe he had been a cruel man after all? How do I know? What is the truth? Is there such a thing as the truth at all, I've often wondered, ever since we – Vanaa, Kishore and I – compared our memories of a childhood event.

I was only nine then (and so, Vanaa and Kishore said, my version of the story couldn't be right, I was too young, I must have later recreated a hazy memory. But I don't agree, my memory is not hazy, the whole incident is crystal clear in my mind) and Kishore, who was fifteen, had just learnt driving, in secret. He wanted to take Vanaa and me for a drive in my grandfather's car. He planned it thoroughly – I can't remember all the details, but I can remember the three of us sitting in the car, Kishore starting it and the sounds boomeranging off the walls of the garage. I can remember Vanaa holding my hand in a tight, hurting grip, letting go only when we were out of the gate and on the road. I look back now and can see us moving noiselessly through an enchanted night in which everything was white, cold and still. Then the car stopped. Kishore repeatedly turned the key in the ignition. Nothing happened.

'You have to get out and push,' he told us.

I was out in a flash, Vanaa followed and we heaved and pushed; but the old monster refused to move.

'Come on, push,' Kishore's impatient voice prodded us.

We panted and struggled. I can remember my feet slipping away from under me, my face coming down once, hard, on the car, squashing my nose, bringing tears into my eyes. But I kept on at it.

53

'I'm going to have a heart attack,' Vanaa said. She looked terrible, her eyes popping out of her head, mouth open, gasping for air. 'Here, feel my heart, I'm going to die.' I burst out crying.

'What's the matter?' Kishore came out. Vanaa had slumped down, crouching in agony.

'Vanaa's having a heart attack.'

'Don't be a fool. Vanaa, what is it, Vanaa . . . ?'

Then I heard it – the putt putt of a motorbike. 'That's your Appa's motorbike,' I said.

Vanaa looked up at that, her face so pale she seemed to be on the verge of fainting. The motorbike stopped; he got off and came to us, his face unusually stern.

'What is it?'

'Vanaa's not well.'

For the first time, perhaps the only time in his life, he ignored Kishore, picked Vanaa up and saying 'Come' to me, strode to his bike. We sat behind him, Vanaa sandwiched between us. 'I'll be back,' he said to Kishore. I looked round and saw Kishore, his face calm and untroubled, standing by the car like a sentry – the car itself looking unreal and ghostly in the moonlight.

The three of us remember the incident differently. Vanaa says I cried but, 'that's because you were scared something had happened to the car and what would your Aju say? Heart attack?' she asks. 'What rubbish! How could I have thought of a heart attack at that age?'

And Kishore, 'Oh yes, I remember, there was no petrol in the car. Your grandfather was a real skinflint, putting in a cup of petrol at a time.' He says we both cried, Vanaa and I, 'But,' he adds maddeningly, 'girls do that all the time, anyway.'

Three people, three different versions of an event, almost three different events. Where is the truth?

Perhaps the fact is that we all of us create our own

truths, shaping them to our needs, in particular the need to be able to live comfortably with ourselves, with those we love and need. And to do this I will have to leave Mira's life alone. I will go on to her poetry; that's less complicated.

PART TWO

But tell me, friend, did Laxmi too,
twist brocade tassels round her fingers
and tremble, fearing the coming
of the dark-clouded, engulfing night?

The corridors are full of people going home. I'm late. We had agreed on five, it's well past that now. I wonder if Vanaa's left, tired of waiting for me. As I clutch the door handle to push it open, I hear the sounds of a woman sobbing. I hesitate and the cries rise to a crescendo. A man walks past me, his hurrying-to-get-home steps not faltering even for a second. I jerk the door open and enter. Vanaa is bending over a sobbing woman, saying something to her. A white-coated doctor, glass in hand, walks swiftly past me and out of the room. Vanaa is holding the woman's body in a tight grip, as if she can stop the woman's cries by the sheer force of her hold. Suddenly the muscles on the woman's neck, which have been standing out like cords, seem to dissolve, the face becomes smooth, the body goes limp. 'She's fainted.'

'Thank God. Urmi, give me a hand.'

Half-lifting, half-dragging the heavy inert body, we heave her on to a bench against the wall. I remove her *chappals* – it's difficult, her feet are swollen as if she's been on them for too long – and settle her on the bench. Vanaa kneels by her side, chafing her hands. The rancid smell of coconut oil comes to us from her uncombed hair.

'Sorry, Urmi,' Vanaa whispers, 'I was just walking out when . . .'

'No problem, we can do it some other time.'

'Would you like to go home?'

'No, I'll wait. What happened?'

'Her daughter's been admitted with a head injury. An accident. Bhaskar says she was raped as well.'

'My God!'

The doctor comes in, a glass of water in his hand, the water slopping over at each step.

'Fainted?' He holds the woman's wrist, feeling her pulse. 'She'll be okay.'

I move away, lifting the chair we overturned when we moved the woman. Vanaa and the doctor hide her from my view, but in a moment I hear her moaning.

'Will you drink some water? Sit up, that's right.'

She drinks awkwardly, the water running down the sides of her mouth.

'Do you feel better now?'

The woman bursts into sobs, the painful sobs of one not used to crying. I can hear the words, 'My daughter' 'my Kalpana'.

'Don't think of it.'

The sobs go on. The woman slumps back on the bench. Vanaa and the doctor exchange looks of helplessness.

'Some more water?'

The woman takes a sip, chokes. Vanaa pats her. She buries her face in her sari.

'Listen to me, woman,' the doctor begins in Marathi, gives up and goes on in English. 'Hell, I wish I could speak the language.'

The woman, making a determined effort, sits up, blows

57

her nose into her sari end. A bit of fluff from it clings to her nostril. Suddenly she turns to Vanaa and cries out, 'It's not true, tell me it's not true, what you – what this doctor says.'

'Tell her it's the truth.'

'What is he saying, tai? Tell him my daughter is not that kind of a girl.'

'Nobody is accusing your daughter . . .'

'Your daughter hasn't done anything, he isn't saying that.'

'It was an accident, a car knocked her down.'

'This doctor has examined your daughter.'

'She was raped,' he says, still speaking in English.

'Your daughter has been . . .' Vanaa hesitates, searching for the Marathi word, gives up. 'Someone has wronged her.'

'It's not true, you people are trying to blacken my daughter's name.'

'Leave it alone, Vandana. I have my report to make anyway.'

'Report?' She catches the word, looks suspiciously at him.

'He has to tell the police.'

'No, no, no. Tell him, tai, it's not true, don't tell anyone, I'll never be able to hold up my head again, who'll marry the girl, we're decent people. Doctor,' she turns to him, 'don't tell the police.'

He looks confused, irritated. 'Look, tell her it's already in the records, I've put it down after examining her. How the chap in Căsualty could have missed it, I can't imagine. She was so badly mauled – thank God she's unconscious.'

'What is he saying?'

'Listen, Bai, this is a police case. The doctor can't tell a lie. He says she must have got hurt when she was struggling against the man.'

58

'If a girl's honour is lost, what's left? The girl doesn't have to do anything wrong, people will always point a finger at her. Doctor,' she turns to him, 'even if it is true, keep it to yourself, don't let anyone know of it, I have another daughter, what will become of her . . . ?'

'Where is your husband?' The doctor speaks in Hindi now.

'He is,' the woman says in Marathi, 'He is,' as if she is willing to concede his existence no more.

'Isn't he here?'

'He came yesterday after I sent word. He sat, he cried, and went away.'

'Doesn't he live with you?'

'No, he has another wife.'

'Well . . .' He turns away, defeated, then speaks to Vanaa. 'I have to go, you deal with this. If I were you, I'd send her home. She's been sitting here since yesterday, I don't know whether she's eaten anything . . .'

'By the way, Bhaskar, this is my sister-in-law, Urmila. And this is Dr Jain.'

We smile at each other. He mutters something and goes out, followed by Vanaa.

The woman, trying to stand up, sways. I support her while she struggles to push her feet back into her *chappals*. I kneel down to help her, but she draws her feet back sharply, horrified. 'What are you doing?'

Vanaa returns. 'Don't go back to the ward now, you go home.'

'My Kalpana . . .'

'The doctors and nurses will look after her. You go home and rest. What's your name?'

'Shakuntala. Everyone calls me Shakutai.'

'Isn't there anyone who can be with you? How many children do you have?'

'Three. Kalpana is the eldest.'

'Don't you have anyone to help . . . ?'

'There's Sulu, my sister Sulu.' The whole burden of her grief seems to suddenly descend on her. 'Oh God, what will I tell Sulu, what can I say to her? She loves Kalpana, she loves her like her own daughter . . . Sulu . . . Sulu . . .'

'I don't think she should go home by herself,' Vanaa whispers to me. 'I'd have gone with her, but that'll make me very late and I promised Mandira . . .'

'I'll go.'

'Will you, Urmi?'

'No problem. But you'll have to ring up Inni . . .'

'I'll do that. Shakutai, Urmi will take you home.'

'Why, tai? Such a fuss. I can go alone. I went by myself to the hospital when Kalpana was born.'

'But today Urmi's going with you. Come back tomorrow. Are you working?'

'In a girls' school. I'm in the Principal's office.'

'Right. I'm here, in this office if you need help.'

The woman makes a mild protest when I wave for a taxi, but she is too dazed, too tired and, maybe, hungry? Even as I'm wondering, should I take her somewhere and give her something to eat, a taxi stops and we get in.

'Are you also a doctor?' she asks me.

'No, I teach in a college. Vanaa, my sister-in-law, is not a doctor, either.'

She is silent, except when she gives directions to the driver. Once she asks me, 'How many children do you have?'

'Only one. A son.' Must they ask this question? Oh God, must they?

'And your sister-in-law?'

'She has two daughters.'

'Why does God give us daughters . . . ?'

'Don't say that!'

She seems astonished by the ferocity of my tone, and

60

sees something in my face that silences her. How long will they continue to torture me, these jagged, piercing moments of grief? We get off the main road into little lanes I've never seen. The road has been dug up leaving an infinitesimally small passage for the cars to go through. People walk past, uncaring of the fact that they're barely inches from the vehicles. We enter a narrow cul-de-sac and the taxi driver stops before a ramshackle building at her instructions. She waits until I pay him off, leads me through the narrow door and down two steps into a courtyard lined on three sides by rooms. The wooden railings of the passage outside the rooms are festooned with washing.

'I'll go now.'

'No, don't.' She holds my hand tightly in her hard, calloused hand until we go to her room. She murmurs something on seeing it bolted.

'Ai . . .'

A girl has come running to us.

'Where were you?'

'In Rani's house.'

'Where's Sulumavshi?'

'She's gone home. She said to send Prakash if we want her. How is Kalpana?'

'Not dead, not alive.' The woman's personality seems to change the moment we enter her room; she becomes confident, authoritative. 'Come and sit here, tai. Sandhya, where is the sheet? I don't know what you do when I'm not at home.'

Mother and daughter spread a sheet on the one bed in the room. She pats it invitingly and says again, 'Sit. And have a cup of tea. I can't let you go without that. Sandhya, what are you staring at? Go and make some tea.'

I try to protest, but the woman insists so vehemently, I give in. The girl is already pumping up the Primus, stealing

61

looks at me in between. The two of them whisper and I know my presence is being explained.

When the tea is ready, the mother sends the girl out. 'Tai, do you know the doctor, the one who can't speak Marathi?'

'No, but Vanaa knows him.'

'Ask her, tai, to tell him not to make that report. Even if it happened, what difference will it make now? Why report it? The only thing that will happen is that our name will be mud. I have these two girls . . .'

'All right, I'll tell Vanaa. But don't you want the police to find out who did it?'

'You think the police will bother about that? They'll just harass us . . .'

'That's not true . . .'

'Ai . . .' Sandhya puts her head round the door.

'What is it, Sandhya? Didn't I tell you . . . ?'

'But Ai . . .'

'I must go. Come in, Sandhya. And look after your mother. Give her something to eat.'

Shakutai gives me an anguished look.

'I'll speak to Vanaa. And where will I get a bus?'

'Sandhya will show you. Go with her, Sandhya.'

We wait in silence until the bus arrives. The moment I get into it I feel an immense weariness, as if my energy has suddenly drained out of me. I drag myself home. The two flights of stairs seem endless and the corridor looms before me, an immense vista. I ring the bell and hear the sound of running footsteps. Kartik opens it, Inni standing just behind him. Their faces change from anxiety to relief. Something comes alive in me at the sight of them. Little shoots of feeling, of pain, begin. For a moment I can't speak.

'You're late,' Inni says.

'Didn't Vanaa ring you up?'

'That was long back.'

'Inni was so worried, Mama.'

'And Kartik hasn't had his dinner as yet.'

'I'll have a bath and come in a minute.'

I make the chapatties and we start on our meal. And suddenly I remember Anu, her little sparrow mouth open to receive the spoon, banging her own spoon on the table, turning her head to follow Kartik as he dances about the room to amuse her, the spoon scraping her cheek . . .

'My daughter . . . my daughter . . .' Shakutai's cry eddies around me.

'What's the matter?' Inni asks.

'Nothing.'

That's not true. I've suddenly realised – what has happened to Kalpana happened to Mira too.

It runs through all her writing – a strong, clear thread of an intense dislike of the sexual act with her husband, a physical repulsion from the man she married. When did it begin? Before marriage? During the girl-viewing ceremony? When he came with his parents to officially 'look' at her? Or did it have its genesis later, during their first night together?

What is it like with a man you don't know? The thought came to me at a 'first night ceremony' in Ranidurg, when one of Akka's numerous nieces got married. I remember how almost sacramental the bed seemed, with its crackling new sheets, the pillows with their frilled, elaborately embroidered covers, and fruits and milk like offerings on a table by the bedside. The couple sat stiffly, side by side on the bed, while the women performed an *aarti*, singing the song in subdued notes. In fact, a funereal solemnity hung over all of us during the ceremony. I could not see the girl's face, for she looked steadily down throughout, but I could see that her hands were trembling uncontrollably. And the back of her neck, I can remember that, looked like a lamb's, waiting for the butcher's knife to come down upon it. And yet, when I saw her with her husband a few days later, she looked – only the clichéd words fit – flushed and radiant.

Yes, it works, most often it works. But for Mira, it didn't. Akka's story tells me much about the man, the intent single-mindedness with which he went about marrying Mira shows me the quality of his obsession for her; but the story leaves out Mira's feelings entirely. There's no clue as to what she felt and did. Was she pleased at first, triumphant at being married at the age of 18 to the first man who 'saw' her? Was she angry that she had to give up her studies? Did she protest, say anything to her parents?

I've scarcely thought of her parents, but now I go back curiously to the family photograph and notice things I hadn't done earlier. The mother, a bulky woman, dressed for the occasion, looks uneasy, sitting slumped awkwardly in her chair, as if she's unused to being centre-stage, and would be more comfortable being in the backgrouund. But the father, a trim, spare man, sits erect, looking eager and alive. There's something jaunty about him that even the solemnity of the occasion hasn't been able to smother. I have a feeling Mira was closer to her father. I imagine that she, his only daughter, was his favourite child. I guess he was proud of her, of her intelligence. And did he guess at her burgeoning talent? Was that why he gave her the book of poetry? Or was it part of his being a school teacher? I wonder too, did Mira speak to her father about her marriage and did he pooh pooh her fears, laugh at her feelings? And did she ever show him the bits she wrote? This, for example, 'Written on my thirteenth birthday'? It gives me the feel of something she wrote for an audience:

'Three little girls playing on the bed, their faces innocent, engrossed, their arms and legs in constant movement. The pillows on the bed have blue borders, Jyotsna is in a blue dress with short sleeves, Bharati is in white and Shobha in a short pink dress that shows her knickers. Jyotsna is the leader as they play one game of make-believe after another. Shobha's excitement as she enters into the game bursts out of her; the other two try to restrain her, but her high voice, her laughter break out of her again and again, even though Jyotsna is stern with her. I write about them and the moment is forever.'

'Forever', the word seems to mock Mira. But does it? I read what she has written and they exist again, those three little girls playing on the bed, Mira in a chair, wearing a crumpled home-wear dress, her legs folded under her, a book in her lap, her eyes dreamy, gazing at the girls, while her mind moves about among the words, choosing the right ones with which to recreate the scene. Yes, she is already a writer, I can see it here, I can see her preparing herself, flexing her muscles, aspiring for eternity. Yet, uncertain too. Questioning herself. Though this poem must be a much later one.

'Huddled in my cocoon, a somnolent silkworm
will I emerge a beauteous being?
Or will I, suffocating, cease to exist?'

She's written about the day a promising young poet, Venu, was invited to her college to speak to the students as if it was a significant event for her:

One of the boys asked him why he chose the name Venu for himself. 'Because,' he said, 'I am that, a flute. The creator of the music is someone else, I am only an instrument.' And how strange, he didn't sound humble when he said that, he sounded almost arrogant. How proudly he declared, 'I am only an instrument'! He read out two of his poems. I've written them down so I won't forget. Each time I read them, I am filled with awe. Will I ever be able to write like this? Today, after hearing

65

him, I know this is what I want – to be able to write like this. But I can't believe I ever can. And, thank God, I never say this aloud. They will laugh at me, I can imagine how they will, I can hear them laughing.

She did write. And, I guess, never showed her poems to anyone because they would laugh. They lay here, in her trunk, until the day we found them and Akka read them. Then, instead of laughter, there were tears.

> But tell me, friend, did Laxmi too
> twist brocade tassels round her fingers
> and tremble, fearing the coming
> of the dark-clouded, engulfing night?

Laxmi. To me, the name conjures up that beautiful figure in the Ranidurg temple, wearing what I thought was my Baiajji's sari, the rich green and gold colours glowing in the light of the dim oil lamps against the dark, polished stone of the goddess.

'Look, Baiajji, she's wearing your sari!' I shot out an accusing hand and Baiajji's tiny fingers covered her mouth, trying to prevent the laughter from breaking through, while the other women gave me reproachful looks.

What memories of her own life did this poem bring back for Akka? Did they say it of her and her husband too? 'A couple just like Laxmi-Narayan'? Or were her tears born of pure pity for Mira, the frightened girl who feared 'the coming of the dark-clouded, engulfing night?' And how was she so sure the experience was Mira's own? *I* know, because it's here, in her diary, the clay out of which she shaped her poem:

Talk, he says to me, why don't you say something, why don't you speak to me? What shall I talk about, I ask him stupidly. 'What did you do today, where did you go, what

66

have you been thinking about all evening?' and so he goes on, dragging my day, my whole self out of me. But I have my defences; I give him the facts, nothing more, never my feelings. He knows what I'm doing and he gets angry with me. I don't mind his anger, it makes him leave me to myself, it is bliss when he does that. But he comes back, he is remorseful, repentant, he holds me close, he begins to babble. And so it begins. 'Please,' he says, 'please, I love you.' And over and over again until he has done, 'I love you.' Love! How I hate the word. If this is love it is a terrible thing. I have learnt to say 'no' at last, but it makes no difference, no difference at all. What is it he wants from me? I look at myself in the mirror and wonder, what is there in me? Why does it have to be me? Why can't he leave me alone?

How clear it comes to me across the years, her cry of rage and anguish, 'Why does this have to happen to me?' Why did it have to happen to my daughter? Shakutai asked me. Why? My own question comes back to me – Why?

'You're late' Inni says accusingly as soon as I step in. 'And where's Kartik? I heard his bus . . . oh, there he is.'

I don't like to think of Inni waiting for the sound of my key in the latch, the sound of Kartik's bus. She seemed so self-reliant once, how did she come to this state? Sometimes she seems almost humble in her dependence; it gives me the same pang her loss of beauty does. As a child, her beauty had embarrassed me; it set her apart from the others, made her look as much a luxury object as the bottles on her dressing table. But now, when I see her losing it, her waist thickening, her upper arms flabby, her skin dry, it saddens me.

'Here, two letters for you, Urmi. And one for you, Kartik.'

67

'From my Baba?' His face lights up and he holds the letter as if it is something precious, but I notice that he does not open it at once. He puts away his satchel, removes his socks and shoes, puts them in their place and only then begins to read. There is something curiously adult about him as he does these things. Was he always so serious? I try to disentangle this Kartik from the child who was part of the Kartik-and-Anu duo . . .

'Rekha's gone for the milk. That girl takes her own sweet time these days . . .'

'Is there enough milk for Kartik? We can have our tea when Rekha returns.'

'I've put a glass by for him.' Inni has followed me into my room, and she picks up the brown paper covered packet I've put down by my bag. 'What's this?'

'It's a picture I'd given for framing.'

'Whose? Anu's?'

'Anu's? Why should I have her picture framed?'

'I thought . . . maybe you wanted to put it on the wall . . .'

'I don't need to put up Anu's picture on the wall.'

'To remember . . .'

'I don't need a picture to remember her, I can remember every bit of her, every moment of her life. How can you imagine I need a picture . . . ?'

To put my Anu on the wall, to place my child among the dead, no more a part of my life, never more part of my world – how dare Inni, how dare she think such a thing! A white-hot rage explodes in me, blinding me, so that Inni's face is a blur. Then it comes into focus and I can see her – Kartik standing by her, holding on to her sari, the two faces alike in their expression of fear. I stop speaking. There is a terrible silence. I walk abruptly out of the room into the bathroom, clutching the cold hard edge of the washbasin to steady myself, gulping in painful, rasping breaths. I splash cold water on to my face and anger drains out of me, leaving me exhausted. I return to my room and sit on the edge of the bed, my legs trembling. It is a while before I can stand up. Mechanically I open the packet and look at Mira's picture. But it is Kartik's face I can see, and Inni's, blanched with terror. I'm a tyrant, I'm turning into a tyrant, they're frightened of me. Kartik frightened of me? The thought is unbearable. I go out, but there's only Inni sitting at the dining table. There's something desolate about her pose.

'Inni,' I say gently, 'I'm sorry, I'm really sorry I shouted at you.'

It's a mistake to apologise to Inni, it only makes her more aggressive. But not this time; I notice she's been crying.

'You think you're the only one who cares, you never think, you never imagine what it is like for me. I was with her the whole day, she played with me, she slept in my bed in the afternoons, it was I who put her to sleep . . .'

I have a vivid picture of Anu, a soft warm mound in Inni's bed, opening her eyes and looking at me, the sudden sharp awareness of my presence in her eyes, the small body scrabbling at the covers, sitting up, holding out her arms, the happy cries . . .

'Inni, don't . . .' I put my arms round her. 'I know, I can imagine, but don't go on.'

She can't stop. 'I've told you many times let's call Shanta back, even if there's no work for her at least I'll have someone to talk to. I know I'm a burden to you, but I'm helpless, I have no one . . .'

She goes on crying. Contrition is replaced by irritation. I try to control myself, to soothe her. The phone rings, but neither of us moves. Kartik comes in and, giving us a look of surprise, picks it up.

'This is Kartik Dixit speaking,' he says. Suddenly his

69

grave face breaks into a smile, his careful, precise speech crumples into a more natural tone. 'Mandira? Yes, she's here, yes, I'll call her. Mama . . .'

Mandira's high shrill voice keeps pouring out of the receiver as Kartik transfers it to me.

'What is it, Mandira? Start again.' I listen to her. 'All right, I'll be there right away. Don't worry, I'm leaving right now.'

'Pallavi's sick,' I hurriedly explain to Inni as I pick up my bag. 'And Mandira can't contact Vanaa. I must go, Inni.' But I have to speak to Kartik first. 'I'm sorry, Kartik, I lost my temper.'

'Did you say sorry to Inni?'

'Of course I did.'

Inni laughs, pleased with Kartik. 'Ring up and tell us how Pallavi is if you're going to be late coming back,' she says.

Mandira, still in her school clothes, her face distraught but tearless, opens the door the moment I ring the bell.

'Oh, Urmiauntie . . .' She clings convulsively to me, then abruptly draws away.

'Where's Hirabai? Isn't she home?'

'No, but I got hold of mummy. Pallavi's in mummy's room, come here.'

I sit by Pallavi, gently wipe her face. 'Sssh, Pallavi, don't cry. Do you want some water?'

'Mummy . . .'

'She'll be here soon. Do you know where the thermometer is, Mandira?'

Mandira, flinging the contents of a drawer all over the place, triumphantly hands me the thermometer.

'How much fever is it?' she asks impatiently.

'Quite a lot. Come on, Pallavi, drink this.'

The bell rings. Mandira's tone tells me it is Vanaa. Mandira brings her, holding her by the hand, as if Vanaa is reluctant to enter.

70

'She's very sick, come and see how hot she is, she has very high fever, Urmiauntie saw it just now . . .'

'Urmi . . .' Vanaa's dazed eyes take me in. 'Thank goodness you're here.'

'Touch her, see how hot she is, she's burning . . .'

Mandira, aggressive, unable to control herself, physically forces Vanaa's hand on Pallavi's face. Pallavi opens her eyes, says 'Mummy' and begins to cry afresh.

'See, she's crying, she's been crying all the time, I kept ringing you up, where were you?'

Vanaa, confused, on the brink of tears herself and dazed by this onslaught, moves to Mandira. 'Mandira, please don't . . .'

'I'm not crying, leave me alone . . .' Mandira shrugs her off. Pallavi makes a whimpering sound. 'And go look after Pallavi,' she snaps at Vanaa.

I decide to take charge. 'Vanaa, don't you have any aspirin?'

'Yes, it's in there . . . My God, who did that?' She's taken in the chaos of the emptied drawer.

'I did it. And now, get angry with me, scold me . . .'

'Mandira, come with me, let's make some tea for all of us. And have you had anything?'

'How could I? I had no time.' The child's tone teeters between gravity and tears.

'Come on, then, we'll get you something.'

'Who's the patient here?'

We turn to the door. Vanaa recovers herself with an effort. 'Oh, Bhaskar, come in.'

'Hello.' The greeting takes in both Mandira and me. 'Fever?'

'Yes.'

'Have you given her anything?'

'No.'

'Okay, let's see how she is. Pallavi, open your eyes, that's a good girl . . .'

'Come on, Mandira,' I urge her out of the room. 'Let's get the tea.'

'For me too, please,' Bhaskar says not looking up. 'No sugar.'

Mandira gradually recovers her control as I begin working in the kitchen. She helps me set out the tray and sits on the counter, kicking her legs, moodily munching some biscuits as she talks.

'You know, Urmiauntie, when I grow up, I'm never going to leave my children to go to work.'

'What will you do?'

'Stay at home and look after them.'

'When they grow up, they'll go away and won't need you. What will you do then?'

'Then I'll go and work.'

'Who'll give you a job when you're that old?'

'I don't care. I'll never leave my children alone.'

I realise I have to speak to her. 'Mandira, your mother doesn't leave you alone. That's why she's kept Hirabai for you. Hirabai is always here, you know she's never gone away like this . . .'

'I don't want Hirabai, I want my mother.'

We can't always have what we want, I think of telling her; but it's not the thing to be said to a child, so I let Mandira go on.

'Hirabai is so bossy, and if I don't listen to her, she says, "I'll tell your mother." As if I'm scared of her!'

When we go in with the tea, both Vanaa and Pallavi seem more composed, though there's something dramatic about Pallavi with a wet compress on her head.

'Thanks, Urmi.'

'Mandira did most of the work.'

'She won't thank me, she thinks I never do anything.'

72

'Nonsense, you've been a very good girl. Have you eaten anything Mandira?' Vanaa is trying to go back to her usual self.

'I had milk, but there's nothing to eat. Hirabai didn't . . .'

'Listen,' Bhaskar puts his cup down, 'why don't you come out with me, Mandira? I'm hungry too. Let's go and have a dosa. Would you like that? I feel like eating a masala dosa . . .'

'But, Bhaskar . . .'

He ignores Vanaa. 'What do you say, Mandira? Will you join me?'

Mandira's face lights up, she opens her mouth to say something, closes it and then says sedately, 'I don't mind. If it's no trouble . . . ?'

'It's a pleasure, Ma'am.' Mandira beams. Only now he turns to Vanaa who's been trying to interrupt. 'We won't be long. Come, Mandira. She'll be okay, don't worry,' he says reassuringly to Vanaa and I wonder which of the two girls he's referring to. When he's at the door he turns and says to me, turning his full attention on me for the first time, 'I'll see you some time.'

The door bangs, there is silence. Pallavi is sleeping, slightly restless, her lips parted. We speak in whispers.

'What a scene!' Vanaa exclaims. 'What will Bhaskar think?'

'That you live a normal family life, what else? How did he turn up?'

'I was waiting for a taxi, you know how it is when you want one badly, there seem to be none. I was getting frantic when I saw him and asked him for a lift . . . You know, Urmi, there was a time when all I wanted was to get married, have children and look after my family. I thought that was happiness. And do you remember all the theories we had about bringing up children?'

'I know.'

73

'And look at me now, just coping from moment to moment. No, not being able to cope – that's the truth. Mandira hates me.'

'Don't be silly.'

'Did you see how carefully she avoided saying anything to me when she left? That little chit, she does it deliberately, she knows she can hurt me. You heard her, didn't you? The kind of things she says to me. Do you think there's something wrong with me, Urmi? Am I such a terrible mother?'

'Rubbish, you're just wallowing in self-pity.'

'But it's true. I can do nothing right. Harish says I'm not firm enough with both of them, Mandira says I neglect them . . .'

'Vanaa, you're tired and upset . . .'

'And that wretched woman!' It comes out of her explosively. She looks guiltily at Pallavi and lowers her tone. 'How could she do such a thing? Just let her show me her face, I'll . . . I'll . . .'

'You won't do a thing, you need her. You won't get a servant as good as Hirabai easily. And she's not irresponsible, you know that. There must be some good reason for her absence today.'

'Mandira doesn't get on with her, it's like tightrope walking all the time. And this thing – Mandira's latest – it really worries me. She keeps saying I shouldn't be working. I don't know who's filled her head with this . . .'

'You dare not blame your in-laws, they've been away nearly six months now. She's an intelligent child, Vanaa.'

'It's worse if she's thought of it herself. Why are these kids so demanding, Urmi? Akka went to work, it was part of my life that my mother was a teacher. I never thought she wronged me by going out, I was proud of her. And I'd never have dared to talk to her the way this child talks to me. I remember once I was angry with Akka, I stopped speaking

74

to her. She said nothing for a day, but the next day she took me into the bathroom and whacked me properly. Imagine me doing that to Mandira! I'd never dare. Urmi, why is it nobody thinks of blaming Harish? He's never around, but it's never his fault. If you ask me, it's all Akka's fault. It's she who filled me up with ideas of a career . . .'

I let her go on, listening silently, offering nothing, not even a smile or a consoling pat. Finally, Vanaa runs out of steam, wipes her eyes, blows her nose and looks shame-facedly at me.

'All over?'

'Yes, you irritating creature, it's all over. But, Urmi, Mandira really worries me. She's got some kind of grudge against me. She's so jealous of Pallavi. Pallavi's small and cuddly, she loves being cuddled, and each time I do that Mandira gets into a rage. And yet, she won't let me pet her. Were you jealous of Amrut, Urmi?'

'No, I wasn't.'

And it's true. I never felt any resentment towards him, though I was an only child for six years.

'He was such a cute, chubby thing, wasn't he?'

I laugh. 'Say that when Amrut's around. Maybe it helped, Vanaa, that we weren't brought up together. We didn't have to compete for our parents' attention.'

'Do you think I should send Mandira to live with Akka? She could go to our school . . .'

'Why don't you, Vanaa? I'm sure she'd love it.'

'I can't.' She is horrified. 'I just can't send my child away.'

'Well, you have to put up with her tantrums then. And stop having them yourself.'

'Don't act superior – just because Kartik is so reasonable.'

'Too reasonable. You know that worries me.'

Even as a baby he was so quiet, it sometimes frightened

me – could a normal human being be so placid? Now I know he is perfectly normal, but I worry about the way he can hold things within himself.

As if Vanaa has read my thoughts, she asks, 'Do we have to go on agonising over the children forever, Urmi? Do you think all parents do this?'

'I don't know. Sometimes I think it's women who take parenthood seriously; men don't, not to the same extent, anyway.'

'Well, well,' Vanaa mocks me, 'that's a nice change. Remember how you once argued with me about maternal feelings?'

It was soon after Kartik and Pallavi were born. We were feeding our babies in the middle of the night. Akka, tired after her day's work, was sleeping, one arm thrown across her face to shield it from the light, Mandira burrowing like a little animal into the warmth of her grandmother's body. I was tired, irritable with the continuous disturbance of my sleep, worried by Kartik's inability to suck vigorously. I could never be sure he had enough milk.

'Sometimes, I think,' I told Vanaa, 'they brainwash us into this motherhood thing. They make it seem so mystical and emotional when the truth is that it's all just a myth. They've told us so often and for so long that once you're a mother you have these feelings, that we think we do.'

'Right then,' Vanaa challenged me, 'let's exchange. If it's nothing, any baby will do. You take my daughter, I'll take your son.'

Instinctively I clutched Kartik closer. Vanaa began to laugh, so hard that her nipple slipped out of Pallavi's mouth and she began to whimper. Vanaa looked at Akka, put out her tongue like a guilty child and helped Pallavi to start sucking again.

'I can still remember what you said that day . . .' Vanaa begins.

The phone rings and she rushes to it, leaving her sentence incomplete. It's Inni. Pallavi is fine, Vanaa reassures her. Yes, Urmi will be home soon, she tells her.

'Don't go until I've had my bath,' Vanaa pleads.

'Hurry up, then.'

I tidy the room, wash up and sit down beside Pallavi. The child is sleeping, her face flushed, her lips parted. I change the compress, a little frightened by the heat of her body. Let Pallavi be all right, let the child be all right . . . To whom am I praying?

'You have to believe in the normality of things,' Papa told me once. 'Otherwise living becomes impossible.'

But, Papa, I ask him now, if you always believe in the normality of things, how do you cope with the abnormal? How did you cope with the fact of your impending death when they told you you had lung cancer? But perhaps lung cancer is normal in a man who smoked all his life. And meningitis in a child of twelve months? Maybe Papa meant it differently. Maybe he meant, 'Have faith that things are normal and they will be normal.' No, it can't be that. Papa didn't go in much for things like faith. I remember how he demolished the story of Babur dying for his son Humayun. I read the story in my history book and it so impressed me I narrated it to him: 'Babur took his son's illness upon himself by praying to God and so Babur died and Humayun lived,' I said in an awed voice. Papa was angry. 'They shouldn't fill your heads with such irrational stories,' he said. 'The truth must have been that Babur caught that illness from his son and, being older, died, while his son recovered.'

I didn't like Papa's version much, I preferred the romantic story in my history book. But now I can see something else in that story. Parenthood makes you vulnerable. Since Anu's death I am haunted by fears – what if Kartik falls ill too? What if he dies? Now, as I look at Pallavi, the same fear clutches at my heart: what if she never recovers?

I have to overcome this. This is no way to live. Or will I learn to live with this fear? There were not many things I was frightened of when I was a child. It was only with Baiajji's death that the knowledge of fear really came to me. It was not a fear of death. Baiajji dead seemed just asleep, her body only a little more rigid than usual, perhaps. I didn't even mind sleeping in our room alone that night. Inni and Amrut were to come the next day and Papa wanted me to sleep in his room, but I refused.

It was that night that the bats came. I had my wash before going to bed, picked up my towel, shook it out, and there was a flapping sound, a strange smell. Something hit me in the face. I panicked, hysterical with terror at the flap of the leathery wings, the horrifying cheep cheep, the damp mouldy smell that seemed to emanate from it. I ran out to Papa and it was he who calmed me down, though it was a long time before I could stop trembling.

But I have no defences at all against this fear which grips me when I think of Kartik ill, Kartik dying . . .

The bathroom door opens and Vanaa, framed by clouds of steam, stands for a moment, wiping her feet on the mat. I can see her in the mirror of her dressing table, a mirror which is slightly distorted, so that Vanaa's figure seems elongated, made to seem even taller by the towel which she's wrapped like a turban on her head. Family resemblance, never very obvious, suddenly surfaces.

'What is it? Why are you staring at me like that?'

'Suddenly you look like Kishore.'

'Well, we share a parent.'

'Don't worry,' Vanaa said when I was leaving. 'I'll be all right.'

No, I don't worry about Vanaa. I've too often seen her

emerge from these moments of despair, cheerful and optimistic once again. She seems to go to pieces, but comes out of it intact and whole. Her resilience is amazing. When she was still in school, she made up her mind to be a doctor. She worked hard, adhering rigidly to her schedule, not letting anything distract her from it. And yet, in the crucial year, she fell short by a few marks of what was then needed, and couldn't get into any medical college. She collapsed. She frightened Akka and me with her total breakdown; nothing, it seemed, could stop her weeping. But in a few days, her equanimity almost restored, she began preparing herself for the career of a medical social worker. It was at that time that Akka said to me, 'I always wanted Vanaa to have a sister. I only have brothers and I know what they are! It always grieved me that Vanaa doesn't have a sister, either. And then you came into our house through that hedge; I've never worried about Vanaa not having a sister since then.'

'Are you sisters?' they asked Vanaa and me in school. 'Is she your cousin?' family friends asked when we went together to invite people to Baiajji's *Chaitra-Gouri puja*, both of us sitting stiffly in the back of Aju's old Ford, instead of in the front with the driver Shankar, to mark the solemnity of the occasion. But there is a greater ease between us than there is between sisters or cousins. I've noticed a kind of tension between sisters, a straining at the bonds, a shame at being too close, too much alike. There is none of that between us.

'I sometimes think,' Inni said to me once, sourly, and with what was surely an unusual perspicacity for her, 'that you married Kishore so that you could be related to Vanaa.'

But she's wrong. I didn't need to be related to Vanaa. In fact, by marrying Kishore, I distanced myself from her; as if she, as Kishore's sister, and I, as Kishore's wife, moved away from each other, Kishore coming between us. We've managed to bridge that gap by silence. After that first outraged reaction of hers when I told her I was marrying Kishore, we've never spoken of him, or of our relationship, Kishore's and mine. No, I'm wrong, there was that night, my wedding night – wasn't it then that our silence about Kishore really began?

Vanaa looked at me expectantly, I remember, when I came out of the room Kishore and I had gone into – yes, it must have been just a few minutes earlier, for Akka and she were exactly where they had been, sorting out some clothes. I saw the surprise on their faces as I walked past, ignoring them. Vanaa's voice, calling out something, followed me, becoming shrill and tremulous with panic when I opened the front door and went out. Then it stopped, abruptly, as if cut off with a knife. When I returned the next morning, she gave me a look, but said nothing. She didn't ask me, not then, not ever, why I walked out on Kishore that way on our wedding night. Nor have I told her.

Perhaps it's natural. A man and a woman, sexually intimate, create a world of their own. There's some kind of a barrier between them and the rest of the world. And yet we speak freely of Harish – of Vanaa's relationship with him. It irritated me terribly at first, her constant refrain of 'Harish says'. She says it less now, but her submissiveness, her willingness to go along with him in whatever he wants, makes me angry.

'You let him get away with too much,' I tell her.

'What do you want me to do?'

'Assert yourself. You don't have to crawl before him, do you?'

'I don't crawl, I do what I want.'

'No, you don't. You're scared of him, yes, you are, I've seen you. You don't even dare to call your daughters anything but Mandira and Pallavi, no, not even when you pet them, because Harish doesn't like baby talk . . .'

I said this when she told me, soon after Pallavi's birth, that they had decided to have no more children.

'Two is enough. But, Urmi,' she said, her face wistful, 'I'd have loved to have had a son.'

'You should have told Harish that.'

'I did. And he quoted population figures at me. And he said, one, surely I'm not the kind of woman who craves for sons, am I? And, two, what makes me think the next one will be a boy? He's right, only . . . I wouldn't have minded taking a chance.'

It was her face when she said that that made me furious. I burst out, 'You let him bulldozer you, you crawl before him . . .'

And there was the day I found her, her sari hiked up, the end tucked into her waist in a workmanlike manner, showing she was girded for action, clearing their bedroom cupboards and lofts so that the painters could move in.

'Why can't Harish help?'

'He comes home so tired . . .'

'You know, Vanaa, what you're going to become, coping with everything the way you are?'

'What?'

'A Superwoman.'

'Good! And doesn't that make Harish a Superman?'

'No, a Superbrat.'

She was hurt; and yet, she didn't say to me, she never has, what she could very well have done, 'It's none of your business'. Papa did that when I interfered between him and Inni. Papa's anger and silence were weapons against which Inni had no defence. At such times, I could sense her constant preoccupation with his feelings, her groping towards him, her hurt when he rejected these overtures.

'You're cruel,' I said once, when he'd reduced her to tears.
'Cruel? Am I cruel, Yamini?'

And then he put his arm round her, a thing he did so rarely in public that it seemed an astonishingly overt sexual gesture. And Inni's face, when he did that, was radiant. I acknowledged defeat. It was Inni's love that defeated me.

'Love!' I can hear Mira's voice, scornful and angry. She never wrote any poems about love. Yes, that is odd, most women poets do. But Mira didn't. There's not a single one about love. Didn't she believe in love?

Oh, go away, you intrusive ghost. I believe in love, yes, I do. Those days in Ranidurg with Kishore – when I remember them I can almost feel their velvety texture, the silky smoothness with which they glided by. Magical.

'Unreal.' It was Kishore who said it. 'This is all unreal.' And he looked at me as if he was pitying me. But I didn't want his pity. Nothing could touch the ecstasy that filled my life. I was fearless, confident, my love gave me immense strength.

But somewhere on the way I seem to have lost that confidence. Now there is fear – the fear of Kishore never returning home, lost in the seas somewhere as one of his friends was; the fear of Kishore turning away from me, a distant look on his face; the fear of his not wanting to come back to me. Yes, that's the thing, that's what I am most afraid of. And I can understand them only too well, Vanaa and Inni; I want to submit too. But I know that if I walk the way of submission once, I will walk that way forever. Yet I never ask him 'why?', when he goes away from me even in our few days together, I never reveal my hurt, my longing to keep him by my side . . .

Fixed forever in our places,
face to face the two of us,
like Siva and his nodding Bull.

I have to laugh. I must tell Vanaa . . . but no, I cannot speak of Mira, of Mira's writing, to her. That is another pocket of silence between us. One can never see one's parent as a sexual being; he or she is merely a cardboard figure labelled 'parent'. I can remember how uneasy it made me sometimes, the palpable attraction between Papa and Inni. This, what happened between Vanaa's father and Mira, is much worse. I know Vanaa's loyalty and so I can never speak to her of what I now know her father to be – a man who tried to possess another human being against her will. Was it her mother who told her 'never to say no'?

Don't tread paths barred to you
obey, never utter a 'no';
submit and your life will be
a paradise, she said and blessed me.

But her will rose up against him and the

no, growing painfully within
like a monster child was born.

He forced himself on her in spite of it; it is out of this that Kishore was born.

I will go home when the sun rises, I have told myself. Now it suddenly does, taking me by surprise. The sea changes colour, the dark greyness lifts off the waves, the light transforming them into a sparkling silver; even the menacing rumble of the waves becomes a silvery tinkle. An old woman having a ritual bath bobs up and down in the water; the head disappears, reappears. Then she hobbles out, her wet sari clinging to her. I must go home. Why am I dawdling here? Wasting my time when I was so looking forward to working in these two days of solitude. A dog, a miserable

83

bedraggled object rootling in the sand, comes and sniffs at my feet. I move from foot to foot to avoid it, but it persists, making desperate sniffing forays. 'Shoo,' I say. It backs away at once before this feeble attack. Its abjectness irritates me. Surely a dog should have more spirit? As if it has read my thoughts, it returns. That decides me. I begin to walk, so briskly that I have gone some distance before I stop and look back at a man who has just passed me. I find him doing the same. Yes, it is Bhaskar Jain. Our hellos clash in mid-air.

'This is a surprise. What are you doing here?'

'Walking. And it isn't surprising. I stay close by.'

'I meant our meeting. I've never seen you here before.' He has begun walking with me. 'Do you come here often?'

'Mostly with the children. And you?'

'In fits and starts. Whenever I see my bulk.' He looks down ruefully at himself. 'How's Pallavi? I haven't met either Harish or Vanaa for quite a while.'

'Oh, Pallavi's fine. In fact, they've gone out for the weekend.'

'Harish! I can't believe it.'

'It was Vanaa's doing.'

'Ah, that's more likely it. Harish was my neighbour in the residents' home. He was three years ahead of me and already a legend then. He never seemed to need to relax and presumed others were the same. It was tough on the juniors working with him. He was an example to me – of what I shouldn't be. I've always told myself I'll never get locked into my work that way.'

'Come on, I'll drop you,' he says, when we get to the point where I have to get off the beach.

'I enjoy walking.'

But he's so determined I go along with him to the car park. He is solicitous, asking me whether I'm comfortable, and do I want my seat pushed back? He folds himself into his seat, grumbling, 'Whoever designed this car had midgets in mind'. He seems to know where to go and I have to direct him only once, when we turn off the main road into our lane. I am ready to thank him and get off, but he promptly gets out and looks at me so expectantly that I have to say, 'Why don't you come up?' He agrees immediately. Once inside the house he looks about with an unselfconscious, ingenuous curiosity that amuses me.

'You're alone?' he asks.

'Yes, my mother and Kartik have gone with Vanaa and Harish. I had work, corrections piled up.'

'Hmm. Your father?' he asks, bending down to look at Papa's photograph, hands behind his back.

'Yes. He died four years back.'

'I know.'

'Make yourself comfortable. I'll get us some tea.'

When I return, he is drumming his fingers on the armrests of the chair. 'Now I know,' he turns to me with the air of having solved a puzzle, 'what's so odd about this place.'

'What?'

'There's nothing of you here. I mean, this doesn't seem like your home, somehow.'

'It isn't. It's my mother's. I live with her . . .'

'I know that . . .'

'Listen, I must ask you about this, "I know" you've been saying. What does it mean? Is it just an expression like "you know"?'

'When I say "I know", I mean just that. I know your father's dead, I know you live with your mother . . .'

'Who told you all this? Vanaa? I can't imagine why.'

'Because I asked her.' There is a pause while I pour out the tea. Then he goes on. 'She's also told me about your daughter – your Anusha. I'm very sorry about that.'

I say nothing. He picks up his tea, sniffs. 'What's this?'

85

'Lemon grass. Inni loves it. We grow it in a pot on our balcony.'

'It smells good.'

There is silence again. Then he puts his cup down with determination.

'I wish I'd known you before your Anusha died.' I give him a level look. Doesn't he realise he's intruding? 'I mean, people change. After such a thing you're never the same again.' He stops for a moment, then continues, looking as if he's surprised by what he's saying. 'I had a twin, a sister who died when I was – when we were – thirteen. It changed all of us – my father, me, my mother most of all. She seems an entirely different person now. I sometimes wonder . . .' He looks at me, as if expecting me to say something, then goes on. 'I can imagine you thinking this is an impertinence, but what I'm trying to say is, I know how it is. And after everything passes – grief, shock, anger, bitterness, I've known all of them – this remains: that life is worth living. Or else, why would death be so terrible?'

I can feel grief welling up in me. I must be calm, I must not give way. I remove my glasses, wipe them, noticing with detachment that my hands are trembling. I put them down gently on the table; as if the small click is a signal, my grief gushes out of me with a frightening violence. I slip down to the floor, put my head on the table and give way. In a while it is over. When I return after washing my face he is sitting exactly where he was, as if he has not moved at all. He is neither awkward nor embarrassed about my breakdown, he behaves as if nothing has happened. There is a greater ease between us.

Only now I speak of Kalpana. 'How is she?'

Oddly, he uses the same words her mother had, 'Neither dead nor alive.'

'And she won't recover?'

'Absolutely no chance. And there's her mother, sitting

86

by her every day, waiting for her to come back to consciousness. She may do that, but . . .' He shrugs.

'But what?'

'Well, what I mean is, I don't expect her to ever come back to normality after this. She may become conscious, she may survive – there are patients who go on and on – but it's only prolonging the agony. By the way, I got your message, about what the mother wanted me to do.'

'Yes, what happened about that?'

'I'm sorry, I'd already met the police officer by then. That was an odd encounter . . . You know, there's something I don't understand. Why is the mother so anxious, frantic almost, about her daughter's marriage? Who'll marry her if this gets known, she keeps saying. Can't she see the girl's condition!'

'It's not just this girl, there's another daughter.'

'How old is she?'

'Twelve, maybe thirteen.'

'And her mother's worrying about her chances of marriage! That's exactly what I can't understand. Tell me, is getting married so important to a woman?'

I have to think. 'Yes,' I say finally. 'For women like her, definitely.'

'Women are astonishing. I think it takes a hell of a lot of courage for a woman like that even to think of marriage. Have you seen her husband – Kalpana's father? No? I have. Well . . .' He lets out his breath in a laugh. 'A poor specimen. Vandana tells me he deserted this woman long back. What has she got out of marriage – except for the children, of course? And yet, she's longing for her daughters' marriages.'

'One always hopes one's children will get more out of life than one has. And women like Kalpana's mother do find something in marriage.'

'What?'

87

'Security. You're safe from other men.'

'Oh, come on . . .'

'It's true. Even if it hasn't worked out for her, it usually gives them that guarantee of safety. It takes much greater courage to dispense with a man's protection.'

'Maybe . . .' he seems dubious.

'But you were saying something about an odd encounter?'

'Oh yes. I spoke to the police officer and he refused to accept my findings and change the first report. You know the Casualty man had put it down as an accident? Obviously he hadn't done a proper examination. Let it remain an accident, the officer said.' He tells me the story and I listen intently. The police officer argued with him. Why make it a case of rape, he asked? She's going to die anyway, so what difference does it make whether, on paper, she dies the victim of an accident or a rape? We don't like rape cases, the man said. They're messy and troublesome, never straightforward. But forget that and think of the girl and her family. Do you think it'll do them any good to have it known the girl was raped? She's unmarried, people are bound to talk, her name would be smeared. For all you know she may be a professional, we see a lot of that. But, if you ask me, the man said, she must have been out with a boyfriend – girls of that class always have boyfriends the families know nothing about it. Maybe after they had a bit of fun she was knocked down by a car . . .

'What about the injuries, I asked him? I'd examined the girl, damn it,' Bhaskar says angrily. 'You could see the marks of his fingers on her arms where he had held her down. And there were huge contusions on her thighs – he must have pinned her down with his knees. And her lips – bitten and chewed. Surely, I asked, no vehicle could have passed over her lips leaving teeth marks? The man laughed at that, he had the sense to give in. Okay, he said, she was

88

raped. But publicising it isn't going to do anyone any good. It's going to mean trouble for everyone – the girl, her family, your colleague who first examined her, us. So I let it go. What the hell, I was just trying to put the record straight. It makes me angry that someone should be allowed to get away with incompetence. And then to say that it was I who made a mistake! Oh well, such things happen, I suppose.'

After he has gone I sit down to make a list of the things I have to get in before Kartik and Inni return. But the paper remains blank. I am thinking of the girl who has the marks of a man's hands on her arms, of his knees on her thighs, and of his teeth, oh my God, of his teeth on her lips. And the mother sitting by her side, waiting for her to come back to the life in which such things were done to her.

There is a very ugly sense of being a voyeur; this girl is not to be stared at. She is so slight that her body scarcely raises the coarse hospital blanket that covers her. Her face is discoloured in patches, the lips, dark and swollen, parted as she breathes. Her arms, symmetrically arranged outside the covers, one strapped down for the IV tube, are pathetically thin, the wrists as small as a child's. There are little nicks on her forearms – healing scars of the cuts her glass bangles must have made. A kind of snore emerges occasionally through her lips, and then there is a slight flutter about her face, as if a breeze has passed over it. Once, her breath comes out almost like a word, and her mother immediately bends over her. 'Bala,' she asks, 'what do you want?' There is urgency in her voice, as if she hopes the question will penetrate to wherever Kalpana is. She waits for a response, the breathing settles down to its earlier rhythm and the mother's hand falls by her side.

I go out into the corridor. While I'm wondering whether

to wait for the mother or to go home, she comes out, her face showing she is still with the girl lying on her bed.

'Let's not sit here,' she says hurriedly. 'I can't breathe here. I feel suffocated.'

She leads me out to the large main corridor and sits down on a bench against the wall. The way she settles herself, shifting to find the most comfortable position, tells me this is her usual place.

'I'm here until visiting time is over,' she tells me. 'The first few nights I slept here; now they tell me not to. There is nothing I can do for her, anyway.' Her face is tearless, she's done with crying. She pulls out a small box from a bag she's carrying. She opens it and asks me, 'You don't mind if I eat my *paan*?'

'Why should I? My father-in-law was a great *paan* lover too.'

'Kalpana used to get angry with me for eating it. And now they say it's bad for you – you'll get cancer, they say. I eat tobacco too. That is even worse, they tell me.'

'If you know that, why don't you give it up?'

'I can't. I tried once, oh not because I was afraid of cancer. If it's written in my fate, I'll get it anyway. I thought I could save some money by giving up this habit. I stood it for only half a day; then I thought I would go mad. I went out, rushing to buy the stuff.' She laughs. 'Kalpana was angry. But this – and tea – are the only pleasures left in my life now.'

She has deftly made a *paan* for herself. She wedges it into a corner of her mouth, swallows a glob of tobacco. The smell of raw tobacco wafts about us. I feel slightly sick.

'You're here every evening?'

'I used to come twice a day. Now I've gone back to work. Our Head bai is good, she allows me to get away an hour earlier for this . . .'

'Isn't there anyone else who can come?'

90

'Who'll come? The children? They've gone back to school, Prakash went back the very next day. Sandhya cried two whole days, now she's back in school, sometimes she forgets Kalpana. I don't blame her, she's only a child.'

'What about your sister?'

'Sulu?' She hesitates. 'She never goes out. And she's looking after my home. She cooks, gets things from the shops – she does everything.' She sighs. 'I'm managing, but God knows how long I can continue like this. The nurse was telling me this may go on and on.' Her eyes go blank, visioning, perhaps, a future of unending misery. 'What will I do? What will *we* do?' Her tone is not helpless, she's trying to imagine what it will be like. 'For a few days, everyone was very sympathetic. But now . . . They all know about it, tai.'

I realise she's referring to Kalpana's being raped.

'People in our *chawl* are talking about it. Even in my school – I sent Sandhya with a leave letter and she said they were trying to get it out of her, what happened to Kalpana. That's why I don't want anyone to come here. I don't want their pity. What's the time, tai?'

With an oddly intimate gesture, she takes my hand, turns the wrist over to see my watch. Her hand is rough, the palm deeply grooved, the nails raggedly uneven. I think of the girl's hands, of the vestigial flecks of red paint on her nails. She must have grown them, shaped them carefully before painting them. Surely she left her marks on the man? But they will have faded by now.

'Time to go. I can't do anything for Kalpana, but when I have to go I feel as if something is being torn inside me. I have to drag myself away. The children will be waiting. You'll come again, tai?'

I don't know why I say 'yes'. 'But, don't call me tai. My name is Urmila,' I tell her.

She is not comfortable with my name. 'Tai' is what she

calls the teachers in school, that is what she keeps slipping into as she talks to me. But over the days, as we sit near the unconscious girl and talk, she learns, hesitantly, to say 'Urmila'.

We sit on the same bench almost every day. Only once our place is occupied by a grief-stricken family, and we move to a bench near the public phone. Our talk is constantly disturbed by people screaming into the phone, the hellos repeated over and over again in a kind of desperation. Shakutai seems unaware of this noise, as she is of almost everything except her own misery. But once, pointing to a peepul tree that has grown to the level of this floor, she says, 'We had a tree like this at home.' She means her village home and I wonder whether it is nostalgia that has made her choose this bench where she can see the tree, and whether, watching the needle-points of the leaves dancing in the sunshine, she goes back to her childhood. Yet she never speaks of the past; it is always the present that absorbs her. And Kalpana.

'She is very smart, that's how she got that job in the shop. Kalpana even learnt how to speak English. People in our *chawl* used to laugh at her, but she didn't care. When she wants something, she goes after it, nothing can stop her. She's stubborn, you can't imagine how stubborn she is.' Pride gives way to resentment. 'And she's secretive, she never tells me anything. She didn't even tell me how much her pay was, can you imagine that? Me, her own mother. As if I was going to take her money away from her! I don't want anything. All I ask is that she help me out. She does, I'm not saying she doesn't, but she grumbles. And, can you believe it, she gives her father money more easily than she gives me. She doesn't grumble at that, even though she knows he will use it for gambling. He has that *matka* madness. It makes me furious. I don't understand her. What has he ever done for her? When he left me for

92

that woman, she was angry with me. Can you believe that, Urmila, she was furious with me! "You drove him away," she said, "you're always angry, always quarrelling, that's why he's gone."'

One day Shakutai suddenly bursts out, 'She's very pretty, my Kalpana.' Her tone is both admiring and wistful. And envious? Can one envy one's own daughter? I am amazed.

'She's not like me at all. When she was born, she was so delicate and fair, just like a doll, I wondered how a woman like me could have a daughter like that. Sulu loved her, she still loves her as if she's her own. As soon as Sulu began earning money she bought things for Kalpana – frocks, you know, pins, ribbons, things like that. And Kalpana too – it was Sulumavshi morning, noon and night.'

This woman too, over and over again she goes back to 'my Sulu'.

'There's always been my Sulu. When I went home after work, tired, hungry and thirsty, Sulu would be waiting for me with a cup of tea, a hot meal. Shakutai, you rest now, she would say, don't do anything. But I've never let her do the hard work, or stay up at night to fill up the water. Once she fell ill, we thought it was TB. But God was good, it was not TB, she recovered. She's still delicate, my Sulu . . .'

She goes on talking. The names Prakash, Kalpana, Sandhya roll off her tongue; but somehow it always goes back to Sulu. She says the name with such love and pity, it is as if it is Sulu who is lying there, unconscious and dying.

I sit and listen, I murmur soothingly, I hold the rough hand in my own, I pat it comfortingly. Perhaps it helps, I tell myself, for someone to listen to her. And perhaps it answers, to a small extent, the question I keep asking myself: 'Why do I come here?'

*

Inni's gone. I try to ignore the bang of the door, the keys she's flung before me, but it's no use. I push the keys off the table and they fall down with a loud jangle. Suddenly I laugh and pick the keys up. I should be used to Inni; by the time she returns, she'll have forgotten everything. But will I? Can I forget she called me mean? The thought hurts. Is she right? Perhaps I shouldn't have reminded her about the telephone bill, 'For the tenth time! Surely you can pay for now, I told you, I'll give it to you later.'

She can't believe I don't have the money, just as it never occurs to her that even our two incomes clubbed together can't run to luxuries like taxis all the time, giving saris to the laundry after just one wear, buying expensive pastries . . .

'You're stupid,' Vanaa tells me, 'letting all that money Kishore sends you pile up in the bank, while you agonise over trifles. Why don't you use it? Now, don't put on your mulish look, I mean it, it makes sense.'

Not to me. She doesn't understand that I intend to live on the money I earn, that I will use Kishore's money only when I have to. And if she can't understand, how can I expect Inni to? Only Kishore seems to realise my feelings. He laughs at me, he calls it my 'kept woman phobia'.

'Oh well, I should be thankful Inni's stopped being forbearing with me, that we're back to our normal relationship. Sometimes I think Inni enjoys these skirmishes, they add some excitement to her life. She looks more vigorous, alive . . . Suddenly it occurs to me that Inni is more aggressive when she's dressed up, with all her make-up on. At home, her face scrubbed clean, her hair bound in a rubber band, wearing reading glasses that are too huge for her face, she looks somehow vulnerable. Interesting, I must tell Vanaa this. Not Amrut, though. He's uncomfortable with any criticism of Inni. He's always been a devoted son, and since Papa's death, he's become more so. Filial

94

piety is gaining on him. I suspected it when he gave up his idea of going abroad and decided to try for the IAS instead, something he'd set himself against earlier. Inni, of course, was delighted, but I was flabbergasted.

'You fool, Ambu, don't do this to please anyone. It's your life. And Papa's dead, you can't please him anyway.'

But who knows, perhaps he'd have done this when Papa was alive if Papa hadn't come down so heavily on him with his expectations. I don't know. It could be part of the devoted son syndrome, after all. I remember how he said to me in Hardwar, when it came to the point of immersing Papa's ashes in the river, 'I can't, Didi, you do it.' And how resolutely he turned his back while I emptied the urn and how he broke down and cried after that, so desolately that I clung to him and sobbed too.

And now he writes, 'Let's not sell the house, Didi, Papa wouldn't have liked us to do it.'

I'm not so sure about that. Papa was not sentimental. I have a suspicion it's Amrut himself, his sense of property asserting itself. 'A man of property now,' he said jokingly when we learnt that Papa had left the Ranidurg house to the two of us. 'And I thought he was going to disinherit me. Remember the day he was talking to us about it and how he turned on me?'

'It was your grin.'

'I wasn't grinning, damn it. It was a manly, understanding smile. I was reassuring him he could depend on me.'

But Papa knew him better. 'I'm leaving you all my burdens, Urmila,' he said once.

'I don't mind,' I'd said. And I didn't. But now, for the first time in my life, I am conscious of a feeling of resentment against Amrut. Why does he have to push everything on to me? 'Balkaka says the company isn't going to renew the lease when it expires in January, and what should he do? Why don't you deal with it, Urmi? Why don't you go there and put poor Balkaka out of his misery? Anything you decide is fine by me.'

Except selling the house. Inni wants us to sell it, I know; but I can't think of it, either. Not as long as Balkaka is living there. I can't say that to Inni, though; to speak of it is to irritate her. She refuses to acknowledge he is part of the family: 'Sakumavshi's grandson? And who's Sakumavshi? A servant.' We laugh at her grande dame manner, but her hostility to Balkaka is real and unshakeable. I guess it's her middle-class prudishness that's offended by Balkaka's link with the family. She considers Balkaka's grandmother, who was Baiajji's father's mistress, a skeleton in the family cupboard, something to be discreetly concealed, not flaunted by calling him 'Kaka'! She was horrified when I told her I knew the whole story, that I'd pumped Balkaka and Papa and got the details from them.

It's a bizarre story, with a touch of the Gothic about it. Or, do I see it that way because I'd just read *Jane Eyre* when I heard the story? And naturally, the madwoman who was Baiajji's mother became, in my mind, Bertha Mason, the first Mrs Rochester. That was how I imagined her, crouching on all fours, growling and glowering through long, unkempt hair.

But, of course, she was nothing like that. She was a shy, withdrawn woman, whose only oddity, that increased with the years, was an unreasonable fear of widows and widowhood. After the birth of her fourth child and only daughter, my Baiajji, the fear finally conquered her. She became convinced that she was, in fact, a widow. She gave up wearing jewels, applying *kumkum* and took to all the rituals of widowhood. When they refused to let her wear the widow's coarse red sari, she remained obstinately nude. At which point she was locked in a room by her husband. And, instead of Grace Poole, there was Sakubai, who looked after the madwoman in her locked room, the baby and her husband as well. Inevitably she became his mistress and had a daughter with him, Balkaka's mother, Saroj.

And then (but, both Papa and Balkaka insisted, not necessarily *because* of this) the madwoman burnt herself. From the few occasions when Baiajji spoke to me of her childhood, I have an impression they were happy together – Baiajji, her father and Sakubai. Sakubai brought up Baiajji with great love; and Baiajji reciprocated by lavishing her affection on Sakubai's grandson, Balkaka. But Inni says he has nothing to do with the family.

I know how Papa felt. The house means much more to Balkaka than it does to us; it's part of his feelings about Baiajji. 'Baimavshi made this my home,' he said to me once. 'She made no difference between me and your father, not once.'

It was to Ranidurg that Balkaka came when he was ill and Baiajji took him in. And it's Baiajji's room he has chosen to retain for himself when we let out the rest of the house. It's to that room I went the day Anu died, though how I got there I cannot remember. Only that I was there in that room, the room I'd lived in as a girl, when Kishore came to look for me.

I can't go there! I suddenly shrink from the thought. Surely, Amrut cannot expect me to do that. But I know I have to. Between the girl who lived in that room and the woman who has lost her child, there is a chasm so deep it seems to me it can never be bridged. Yet that was me and this is me too – I cannot get away from that.

Yes, I have to go, I will go to Ranidurg, I will write to Balkaka and tell him I will be there and settle things about the house. And there's something more I have to do. I have to see Mira's house. No, not Mira's house, but the one she lived in after marriage, until she went to her father's home to have her baby and die.

*

97

I have seen Mira's house – the thought startles me, pushes up a memory I never knew existed. I'd gone there with Vanaa to give a message from her father to her uncle. I can remember the house opening directly from the street and the large stone slab, a bridge over the smelly gutter that ran on both sides of the road, rocking as we stepped on it. And the hall, where we waited, a windowless room with an open skylight above that let in both light and air. I can remember how low the wooden-raftered ceiling seemed, even to the child that I was, and the two wooden pillars in the centre, on one of which hung a calendar from a long nail. I saw no more of the house, because it was there in the hall that we waited while Vanaa's uncle came out to us.

Now I have gone into the house once again with Mira. I have seen the corner room where the women sat three long days, sequestered from the rest of the family, the room with a window which looks out on to the street – 'My companion for three days, window in the corner room' Mira calls it. When I read the poem I can see Mira sitting on the floor, hair dishevelled, wearing an old sari, her plate and glass by her side. I can see her drawing herself into a huddle each time someone entered, tucking her sari under her feet, drawing it tightly round her shoulders when the children ran in, afraid of polluting them with her touch. And then, when she was alone, looking out of the window, listening to the cries of the hawkers . . .

> *Shall I surrender to this Maya-world*
> *dancing peacock, displaying its feathers?*
> *Or shall I, defying the market world*
> *retreat into my shell tortoise-like?*

'I can't understand what they're saying,' Baiajji whispered to me in an aggrieved tone on the one occasion she came with Vanaa and me to see an English movie. She was all the more resentful because, as she had often told me, when Aju suddenly decided that his status required his wife to know English she had been taught the language by an Englishwoman.

At first she had resisted, Papa had told me later. 'And I don't blame her. It was the third time she had to learn a new language. Her father made her switch from a Kannada school to Marathi – he thought it meant a chance of a better husband. Yes', (in sharp rejoinder to my involuntary laughter) 'it's true, she said it herself. Then, she went on to Hindi – that was her response to Gandhiji. And after all that, Dada wanted her to learn English. Poor Bai.'

When she spoke to me of it, time had already softened the resentment, and she spoke nostalgically of Miss Taylor and her English classes.

'Taylorbai never spoke like this,' Baiajji hissed in my ears. I didn't tell her then that the American accent defeated me too; but, using the context, I could guess at what was being said. Now, in the same way, I use Mira's diaries to understand her poems better.

Only the poems, I had told myself, I will read only the poems; but it has not been possible. The poems themselves have led me to her diaries and there are passages in the diaries that take me back to the poems. How could I have been so naive as to imagine that I could keep her life and her poetry apart? The diaries and the poems complement each other, the gaps in one are filled by the other. But it's curious how little she mentions the family she married into. She lived with them, yet of her life there, apart from a few hints, there is nothing. I prise out some facts from the poems and hoard them in the trunk labelled 'Mira'. I can see she was lonely.

They called me mad
they, who cocooned themselves

99

in bristly blankets
and thought themselves warm
when I spoke of my soul
that boiled and seethed.

They called me mad
they, who were entranced
by a single white ray of light
when I spoke of the magic
of the seven colours in a prism.

I remember how Vanaa, who had known Harish for two
years before she married him and had come to know his
family too, had thrown herself at me, sobbing, as soon as
she saw me, the first time I visited her after her marriage.
'I'm all right,' she said, swiftly recovering and wiping her
eyes. 'I'm all right. They're all very good people, but . . .'
She could not explain. 'You'll know when you get married
yourself,' she said at last.

But I never did, because I married Kishore, whose
home, whose family, had been like mine since I was a child.
I never knew this feeling I saw on Vanaa's face, I see in
Mira's poems.

As if born blind, I grope
finding my way in a new world
touching things feeling them,
oh, what is this, so strange and new?

The sun sets, the lamp unlit,
wrapped in my cloak of darkness, I sit.
What is it that flutters there?
Is it the glowworm, is it the moth?

But loneliness was, perhaps, a part of Mira's being.
There's that family photograph in which she stands a little

100

aloof from the rest of them. The youngest brother's hand is on his mother's lap as if for reassurance, the other boy stands close behind his mother, but Mira is distant – and not just physically.

I remember the day the astrologer came home. He read all our horoscopes, told us our futures and we listened as if they were stories about other people. Only my mother's horoscope was not read. 'Don't you want to know your future?' I asked her. And she said – I remember she was serious when she said this – 'What's there in my life apart from all of you? If I know all of you are well and happy, I'm happy too.' Did she really mean that? Will I become that way too, indifferent to my own life, thinking it nothing? I don't want to. I won't. I think so now, but maybe my mother thought like me when she was my age. It frightens me. No, it doesn't, I'll never think my life, myself nothing, never.

They named her Nirmala on marriage. That's the name I knew her by at first. Kishore's mother, Nirmala.

A glittering ring gliding on the rice
carefully traced a name 'Nirmala'.
Who is this? None but I,
my name hence, bestowed upon me.

Nirmala, they call, I stand statue-still.
Do you build the new without razing the old?
A tablet of rice, a pencil of gold
can they make me Nirmala? I am Mira.

PART THREE

The wheel of seasons turns,
the monsoon river flows turbid and red,
the lightning flashes its splendour,
the rainbow arcs in celebration,
all things are as they were.
Only I, unmoving, becalmed,
have changed.

It is a Saturday evening and leisure seems to unroll before us as we sit and watch the children playing in the sand. They are absorbed in their game. Pallavi sits still in a kind of martyred dignity, one leg stretched before her. Kartik, spurred on by Mandira, digs energetically and gets her the sand which she pours and pats into a mound on Pallavi's foot. 'Don't move,' she warns Pallavi each time, as she shapes the mound to her satisfaction. But Pallavi, suddenly tired of being still, slumps from her statuesque pose, twitches her leg. The edifice crumbles, disintegrates. Mandira slaps her smartly, Pallavi begins to cry and runs to us. She sits on my lap, using me as a shield, while Mandira and Vanaa argue.

'Really, Mandira, must you lose your temper so fast?'

'Look, mummy, how she spoilt it, I was going to make such a wonderful castle . . .'

'Anyway, that's a stupid game. Stop digging, Kartik. God knows what rubbish there is under that sand. Go and play something else.'

'We don't want this crybaby.'

'I don't want to play with you.' Pallavi settles herself more comfortably on my lap.

'Come, Pallavi,' Kartik urges.

He waits for a moment but Pallavi ignores him and so he goes after Mandira.

'Honestly, Vanaa, you're the limit – telling the children the sand is dirty. You'll soon be asking them to wash it before they touch it!'

'This is Bombay sand. And isn't it muckier than usual today?'

'That's because of Coconut Day . . .'

'But that was – when? Wednesday? Or was it Thursday?'

'Anyway, it means the monsoon is over. Almost.'

'What do you mean over? It's only August. How can it be over? Coconut Day means the monsoon is really beginning.'

We argue about it. 'I thought the coconut offering was a kind of propitiation,' Vanaa says.

'No, thanksgiving. It means the worst is over.'

'Yes, the worst is over.'

We fall silent. Pallavi, bored with us, runs off to join the other two.

'Do you remember, Urmi, once in Ranidurg we were sitting in the college gardens and a chap began to sing . . .?'

'What day, what chap and what song? How do you expect me to remember such a vague thing?'

'We were still in school then, and the song – I think it was a Meera bhajan – I can't remember which one . . . Why, how extraordinary, I've suddenly remembered.'

She begins to hum in her husky voice, '*Sakhi*, why do I need *kaajal* when I have *Ghanshyam* in my eyes?' and then, suddenly self-conscious, stops. We laugh.

'Isn't it odd the way it came back? But what I was going to say is, the reason I remember that evening is because that was the first time I fell in love. With that boy. Maybe it was his voice, or the evening or – well, I don't really know. But for days I used to dream about him.'

'Vanaa, you never told me!'

'You were such a kid, I couldn't possibly talk to you of love! Inniauntie would have . . . What's the matter?'

'I've suddenly remembered. Inni might call up tonight. She doesn't know we're going to your place.'

'When is she returning?'

'I don't know. You know what Delhi means to her. Remind me to ring her up as soon as we get home.'

'I want to talk to her too.'

'I bet you'll ask her, "What did you wear to the party, Inniauntie?" And then you'll say, "You must have looked lovely, Inniauntie." Honestly, Vanaa, you're such a smarmy hypocrite with Inni.'

'Don't be rude. I think she's lovely, really I do. When I first saw her . . .'

'I've heard all that before. And I was speaking of your behaviour with Inni the day before she left for Delhi. I heard your conversation – she was complaining about me . . .'

'Not complaining, Urmi, she's worried about you. Your visits to the hospital, you know. She can't understand what you have to do with Kalpana and her mother. And the way you lock yourself into your room when you're at home . . .'

I suddenly flare up. 'And am I supposed to go on and on in the same way forever – go to work, do the shopping, the cooking . . .'

'You don't have to. You know Shanta is willing to return any time. She will relieve you of all the drudgery.'

I ignore her. 'Manage everything, including money and . . .'

'Peace, peace.'

104

I take a breath and laugh. 'Oh well, I've taken it on myself, I can't complain. But Inni shouldn't either.'

'She wasn't.'

'She was. And all that you could say was, "Yes, Inniauntie" and "No, Inniauntie" and "That's right, Inniauntie."'

'What do you expect me to say?'

'Couldn't you have said, "Inniauntie, Urmi is my friend and I can't listen to any complaints about her" . . . What's the matter with you, you idiot?'

'Really, Urmi, you're too absurd. Just imagine me saying, "Inniauntie, Urmi is my friend . . ."'

She can't go on. She breaks into spluttering, uncontrollable laughter once again. And stops for a moment to find me staring sternly at her.

'Smile, child, smile,' she says. 'You look like your grandfather when you're like this.' And then she starts off again.

Bombay affords a person total privacy. You can cry, laugh, bathe, cook, eat, even die in public – and very few people will turn round and stare. But now a woman passing by gives us a curious look, then stops.

'Urmi?' she asks hesitantly. Then more confidently, 'You are Urmi.'

I look up at a plump smiling face. It takes me a moment to connect this woman to her younger, slimmer self . . .

'Lalita.'

'Took you some time, didn't it? But I knew you right away.'

I introduce Vanaa to her and Lalita begins to tell me about herself, filling in the blanks since we last met. Vanaa, mumbling something, wanders away. Lalita scarcely notices her.

'And my sister died last year, her baby is with us. The baby's real cute, but it's hard managing I tell you, what with my job and Ashok touring 20 days in a month . . .'

Finally she stops for breath and looks at me. I realise she's waiting for me to offer her my history in exchange. I hesitate and – I should have known this would be her first question – she asks me 'How many kids do you have?'

'Only one. A son.'

Her look is like a nudge, telling me to go on, but our conversation falters. She senses something perhaps, for after exchanging phone numbers and promises to meet she goes away.

Only one, a son . . . the words keep hammering in my mind. How could I, oh God, how could I? That was betrayal, treachery, how could I deny my Anu? I can feel the grittiness of the sand under my palm as I push my hand deeper into the sand, pour more sand on it, smoothing the sandy ridges flat, patting it into shape, angry little pats that hurt and are somehow satisfying. Only one son . . . how could I?

I pull out my hand with a jerk and the mound collapses into a ruined heap. I am looking at the debris when I see Vanaa returning, marshalling the children before her, an anxious, 'We're late' look on her face.

'Who's going to drive?' Vanaa asks when we get to the car. 'You or I?'

Mandira looks from face to face and says with a judicial authority, as if the question was addressed to her, 'You drive, Urmiauntie.'

I laugh, the hard knot in my chest dissolves.

'What's wrong with my driving?' Vanaa wants to know, suddenly belligerent.

'Urmiauntie drives better.'

'She drives like a maniac, but if you prefer that . . .'

'Urmiauntie,' Pallavi calls out from the back, 'you and Kartik are coming to our house?'

'Yes, Pallavi.'

'Where will you sleep?'

'Wherever your mother tells us to.'

I've no doubt Vanaa has it all planned and arranged. Actually, it's Harish's sense of order and perfection which is the rock on which Vanaa has built her life.

'It's a reaction,' Vanaa told me once, with the humour-lessness that any mention of Harish brings out in her, 'to his mother's total lack of order.'

If so, will Mandira and Pallavi become sluts to get away from their mother's obsessive orderliness? Reluctantly I abandon this fascinating thought and listen to Vanaa who has got herself into a state.

'It's late,' she keeps repeating.

'For what? There's no one waiting at home, is there?'

The way Vanaa says 'dinner' it seems as if Harish, in Baroda, has some kind of remote control over her; as if not to have dinner at the time set by him would be fatal.

'Relax, Vanaa, the kids have just had ice cream.'

But Vanaa can't relax. The moment we're home, she begins harrying the children. 'Put those dirty shoes away, I don't want sand, for God's sake, all over the house. And have your baths and change before you come into the kitchen . . .'

When the children retreat before the storm, she starts on Hirabai, furious that she hasn't yet made the beds, that the puri dough is too soft . . .

'God, Vanaa, you're in a real nit-picking mood.'

'You can laugh, but it's impossible to get puris the right shape when the dough is so soft.'

'Give me the puris. I will shape them. You get on with the potatoes.'

'Okay. Mandira, if you've changed, come and set the table.'

'I'll do it if you don't interfere. I don't want your conditions.'

107

'Do it right, that's all I ask. And oh God, I forgot the jelly, I'll do that first.'

'Auntie, let me stir,' Kartik begs.

Kartik is vigorously stirring the red liquid, lips parted, tongue showing, forehead wrinkled in earnest concentration. I drag my eyes away from his face. I mustn't look – the evil eye. I remember Baiajji pointing to a growing plant with her knuckles. 'If you point a finger at it, it will die.' And putting a black dot on Amrut's cheek after his bath, 'To ward off the evil eye'. 'A mother's look is the worst' someone used to say. Did I do that to Anu? Is it because of me . . .?

Rubbish, rubbish! What's wrong with me? What nonsense am I thinking?

'Auntie, auntie,' Pallavi is pleading, 'he won't let me do it. Kartik, I want to stir, tell him no, auntie.'

'Never mind, Pallavi, you help me to shape these rounds for the puris, come on, that's a good girl.'

'Auntie, you're partial.'

'Why, Mandira?'

'You should take Pallavi's side because Kartik is your child. Mummy always takes Kartik's side.'

'Fantastic logic, but I don't take sides.'

I roll out the first puri and slip it into the oil. It sinks heavily to the bottom of the pan, then floats serenely to the surface.

'There!' I say triumphantly. 'Does the shape matter?'

Vanaa makes a face at me. Pallavi, standing on her toes, asks, 'Urmiauntie, is that my puri?'

'Yes, look how it's puffed up.'

'My puri's puffed up, my puri's puffed up . . .' She dances round the room, chanting, blowing out her cheeks. Kartik and Mandira, infected by her excitement, join her and the three children prance about the room, laughing, singing, dancing. For some moments there's pure chaos. The pain pours out of my eyes. Anu . . .

'Urmi, can the children start?' Vanaa calls out from the dining room.

'Yes,' I shout back, furiously rubbing my face on my shoulder and go on with my rolling.

There's a slight sense of disorientation when I enter the ward and find Shakutai by a bed at the other end of the room. Have they moved Kalpana? No, it's Shakutai who's gone to help a young woman with a paralytic patient. I can hear her encouraging murmurs as they heave the heavy body on to a side. She vigorously slaps the dead flesh, the sounds fill the room.

Standing by Kalpana, I notice how the contours of her face have changed, the bones pushing themselves against the parchment-like skin. There's a kind of deathly stillness about the body, the face almost a mask in its rigidity.

'There's nothing I can do for her now,' Shakutai says when she joins me. 'That's why I thought I'd help that girl. It's her mother – the girl is frightened, she's never seen illness before. They came here only yesterday. That one,' she points to a bed, 'she's being sent home tomorrow. Well,' she sighs, 'I might as well go home.'

'Come home with me,' I say on an impulse.

She demurs, but I insist. Perhaps the fact that Inni is away makes it easier for me to persuade her; Inni, I know, would be uncomfortable with such a guest. When we get home, I realise that Shakutai is just as uncomfortable being my guest. She perches herself awkwardly on the edge of a chair in the living room, swivelling her head uneasily away from her image in Inni's decorative mirror on the wall.

'Come into the kitchen with me. I'll make us a cup of tea.'

'So much trouble,' she murmurs, but she follows me in

109

with alacrity. Here she looks more comfortable. She asks me about Inni, Kartik, about who cooks for us, who does the other work. Her gaze travels about the kitchen, taking in everything.

'This was one of my dreams, to have gas to cook on. It makes cooking easy, doesn't it?'

'Very.'

'And my other dream was to have this,' her hand goes to her neck, where her string of black beads has sunk into the creases in her throat, '*mangalsutra* made in gold. Then one day I thought – the man himself is so worthless, why should I bother to have this thing made in precious gold? That's been the greatest misfortune of my life, Urmila, marrying that man.'

I make the tea and as we drink it and wash up, she tells me about her marriage. She has a loud voice – she is used to speaking against noise – but it drops to a whisper when she comes to something she considers 'delicate'.

'They told us, when I married him, that he would soon take me away to Bombay. I waited six months, almost a year, then I decided to go myself. My father was not a rich man, how long could I burden him? So I went. And the day I came here, I knew the truth; this man had no job. Not that he couldn't have got one, but he didn't want to work; not all the time, anyway. He would take temporary jobs, then idle for months. He was living with his cousin-brother who's in the police, they had a room in the police *chawl*. They didn't mind my joining him, why should they? They had a free servant to drudge for them. I didn't mind working, I'm never frightened of work, I'm used to it. I did all the work without complaining. But . . .'

What she minded the most – I can see the anger in her eyes even now when she speaks of it – was that they made the couple sleep in the common passage outside their room.

'I, a woman, had to sleep there, in public, with strange

110

men walking up and down. And my husband . . .' the voice drops low 'you know what men are, he wanted to . . . We're not animals, I told him. As if he cared. And I got pregnant. It was the worst thing that could happen to us then. I'd just begun working in a grocer's shop, just started earning some money, and this happened. I didn't want the child, I didn't want Kalpana, I wanted her to die.'

She sees my face and flashes out at me. 'You can't understand, you won't understand, how will you? I took things, I used to hit myself hard – here – with the rolling pin, you understand, when making chapatties – but nothing happened. She was born.' She is silent for a while.

'It was Sulu who comforted me. I called Sulu to help. And she said, "Look how pretty she is, Shakutai, just look at her." I don't know what I'd have done without Sulu. She looked after Kalpana, then Prakash, and then Sandhya while I went to work. I've done all kinds of work, Urmila.' She holds out her hands to me, as if in proof of her statement. 'I never minded any of it. I even looked after a paralytic old woman for a year, cleaning up her filth.' Of course, that is why she had been able to handle the patient in the hospital so expertly. 'I did it all so that my children could grow up, that they could go to school, live better than me. And that's why when Sulu and her husband said they would keep Kalpana with them, that they would look after her schooling and everything else, I was so relieved. It was a God-send for me. But Urmila, that girl ran away from them in just three days. She went to her father – can you imagine that? To her father and that woman. He brought her back here of course, catch her letting Kalpana stay with them. And then Kalpana refused to go back to Sulu's house. I argued with her, I scolded her, I beat her, but it was no use. She wouldn't go back. "Die then," I said, "What do I care? What can I give you but dry chapatties and one set of clothes?" Whereas Sulu – what would she not have done for her?'

111

Suddenly it bursts out of her. 'Sometimes, Urmila, I think I was cruel to the girl; but I did it for her. I wanted her to have all that I never had – education, a good life, a good marriage, respect from others. Look at me – what am I? I don't want my children to be like me.' And then the cry breaks out of her. 'Did I do wrong, Urmila, was I cruel to her?' And again, 'I didn't want her to be born, is that why she's dying now? Is this my punishment?'

I listen to her with a strange feeling of 'I've heard this before'. Then it comes to me. It was Papa. I've seen this in Papa. The same morbid self-questioning, the same ancient guilts surfacing.

'We wronged you, Urmila,' Papa cried out to me.

That was a weird conversation we had – this was in the early stage of his illness. He was wholly unlike himself then, uncharacteristically self-doubting, with a sense of having wronged everyone.

'We wronged you, Urmila. No, I shouldn't say "we"; it's my fault entirely. Yamini always left all the decisions to me. I shouldn't have sent you away to Ranidurg, I should have kept you with us.'

'But, Papa, I was happy there, I was very happy with Baiajji.' It is true. It was Baiajji who made me feel privileged; I realise that now. I was loved and wanted. Even her scrupulous sense of fairness – if she cut a mango, she would give a piece to everyone in the house, including the servants – deserted her when it came to me. I was always special to her. Love, I know it now, is the greatest enemy of egalitarianism.

I tried to convince Papa about this, but failed. He refused to be convinced. He dredged things out of the past to scourge himself with, things I hadn't even thought about.

'I shouldn't have left you alone with your Aju after Bai

112

died,' he confessed another time. 'That was no situation for a child of fifteen to cope with.'

'We'll manage by ourselves, won't we?' Aju had asked me.

'Yes,' I said, 'we'll manage.'

And we did. It was not easy, I soon realised; but I couldn't tell Aju that. 'Are you all right?' he used to ask me. 'Yes,' I would reply; it was as if, after living with Baiajji for years, I'd got her antenna which could pick up Aju's real feelings, so that I knew what it was he wanted me to say. 'Yes, I'm all right,' I would say, and I could sense the relief with which he turned away.

'It was to be for just a month or two,' Papa went on, apologising, it seemed, for what happened years back. 'I wasn't going to leave you two by yourselves for long. I was going to take you both away.'

Aju didn't want to go. He was terrified at the thought of leaving his home, of living in a strange place. Papa wouldn't have liked to be told this; to admit it would be to admit the fact that Aju may have died to avoid leaving his home. And so I said nothing. But when he cried out against himself for having let me have my first baby in Ranidurg, I protested.

'Papa, that's stupid. You know you couldn't help it, Amrut had hepatitis . . .'

'We should have sent him somewhere, we should have done something. We failed you as parents by not looking after you when Kartik was born. It was wrong to let your mother-in-law do it.'

I know it would have hurt him immensely if I had told him how right it had been for me to have my baby in Ranidurg, how happy I had been then. It was not just the innocent euphoria of a first pregnancy ('tiny fish swimming in the ocean of my womb/my body thrills to you' – yes, Mira knew how it was) it was being there with Vanaa and Akka, having them to help me. If he couldn't understand

113

my feelings about Baiajji, how could he realise the way I felt about this? They seem to me, even now, like an idyll, those two months we spent in Ranidurg, Vanaa, Mandira, the two new-born babies and I – with Akka the matriarch who looked after us all. Nothing existed but our physical needs, and those were all fulfilled. It was a primeval, innocent world.

But it was no use telling Papa this. He was in no mood to condone himself. He wanted to beat his breasts, to cry out '*mea culpa*'. It surprised me, this trait in Papa. Was it his illness? But he had been so pragmatic about it earlier.

'Take them back,' he'd said when I'd given him the two shirts I'd bought him. 'Or exchange them for Kishore's or Amrut's size.'

'But Papa, I bought them for you.'

'To wear just once or twice? I have no time to get through even the ones I have.'

'Papa, you're being morbid. And ghoulish.'

'No, realistic. I can't close my eyes to the truth. I have bronchogenic carcinoma.' He'd said the words easily and naturally. 'And, if you want to do something for me, promise me one thing. No heroic life-saving treatment for me. I'm depending on you.'

Yes, he was very matter-of-fact. But now I know it was just a blind. He was terrified, he didn't want to die. He made his will, wound up his affairs, but he was never really prepared for death. No one can ever be. I could see it in the way he changed. At first he had been full of love and tenderness for all of us. I can remember his face when Inni broke down after she was told the truth about his illness; it was overflowing with pity for her. Later, as if he needed to save up all his emotions for himself, he became disinterested, withdrawn, his attention turned inwards, absorbed in the process of his own death. He was morose and irritable. When we tried to involve him with routine life, he turned away with great weariness, as if saying, 'Why do you bother me? Leave me alone.'

And then he changed again. He came back to us, but he seemed to be looking for some reassurance none of us could give him. There was panic in his hand that gripped mine hard, there was anger in his eyes when we spoke of ordinary everyday things in his presence. What did he want from us? None of us knew, none of us could help him. Dying is a terribly lonely business. And so he turned his face to the wall and died. Kalpana is spared this. But perhaps her mother is enduring all that on her behalf. I've seen it in her mother's eyes, the same fear of dying, the same longing for death that I saw in Papa's. Is that what the living have to do – to carry the burdens of the dying and the dead? I have Baiajji's silver pins, her saris, I have Mira's bangles; none of these things means much to me. But when I read Mira's papers, something comes through. It's like a message being tapped on the wall by the prisoner in the next cell. She's trying to say something. What is it?

Inni, hovering near the door, says it again as I check my bag to make sure I have the keys. 'You won't be late, will you?'

'No, Inni, I told you Bhaskar will drop me home. You just don't have to worry.'

She opens her mouth to say something, closes it again. Her uneasiness is palpable. She doesn't like my going out with Bhaskar; nor does Vanaa. 'Do you expect me to live like a cloistered nun just because I'm married?' I asked Vanaa irritably.

'It's not that, but . . .' She didn't go on.

'It's just an evening out, don't take it so seriously, Inni,' I want to say to her. But even to say this seems to give the occasion more significance than it has.

'Have a nice time, Mama,' Kartik calls out to me from his room.

'Thank you, darling.'

I go down and join Bhaskar, my mood suddenly lighter. Bhaskar too is in a flippant mood. He won't tell me where we're having dinner. He's like a child with a secret.

'Here,' he says finally, stopping the car. 'You don't like the place?' He turns to me at my sudden exclamation, his face crestfallen.

'It's not that, I've never been here. It's just that this place is supposed to be shamefully expensive. Isn't it?'

'Oh,' he cheers up, 'that's all right. I can afford it.'

'I never knew resident doctors were paid so well.'

'It's my father who has the money.' He's very matter-of-fact about it.

'When I take you out,' I tell him after we've settled down, 'don't expect anything like this. You'll have to put up with what I can afford.'

'No problems,' he says cheerfully.

While he gets absorbed in a serious conversation with the waiter about our dinner, I wonder why I said that about taking him out and how easily he accepted it. His naive pleasure also makes me wonder whether this is the first time Bhaskar has taken a woman out for dinner.

'The food is good here,' he assures me after we've ordered our meal.

'Good.' I smile at his earnestness.

'You think I'm greedy, don't you? I am. And you . . .?'

'I'm spiritual. Above such gross matters like food.'

'Ha! What's your birth sign?'

'Birth sign? Oh, you mean . . . I'm a Leo.'

'A Leo? Why, I'm a Leo too.' He is animated and goes on to discover that there's just a week between our birthdays. He seems to find the fact interesting. And exciting.

116

'Do you believe in these things? I mean, stars, birth signs and all that?'

'I don't know. But I enjoy reading the forecasts. My mother initiated us into it. She was a great believer. Well . . .' he is suddenly hesitant, 'I thought she was.' He leans forward, earnest now. 'But I believe in personality types. Don't you?'

'What types? You mean, because we're both Leos, we have the same kind of personality? Tell me, are we alike?'

'How do you know we aren't?'

The look of belligerence on his face emphasises the 'boxer's look' which his snub nose and rather muscular, stocky figure confer on him.

'My sister now, she was a real Leo. She loved to command, to be the centre of attention. But maybe that was the result of her being my mother's favourite. The household revolved round her.' He says it without a touch of rancour.

'She was the one who took decisions, between the two of us, I mean. She was quick, while I dithered. I knew that ultimately I'd reach the same point she'd done earlier, so I left it to her.'

'Which means you aren't a real Leo after all.'

'No, no, you don't understand. We were twins, you see, so we shared that quality between us. She had a greater share of it, that's all. And after she died, it all came to me. It began the moment she died.'

He looks reflectively at me, but it's not me he's seeing. Something has happened to his face. All the features look softened, almost blurred.

'I've never spoken of this to anyone, but I knew it, the moment it happened, that she was dead.'

The waiter comes to light the candle. We are silent while he does it, but the moment he turns away, Bhaskar calls him back. 'We don't want this . . .' He turns to me. 'Do you?' I shake my head. 'Take it away,' he tells the waiter.

Bhaskar waits until the man has gone before resuming. 'I was home that day. Both of us had had the flu. She'd just recovered, but I wasn't fit enough to go to school. My mother didn't want her to go either that day, but Jyoti was adamant. She went.' He falls silent. 'She was knocked down by a bus on her way home.' The words seem to be propelled out of him. 'I was in bed and suddenly there was a kind of blankness in me, about me, I was lost in that blank nothingness . . . no, I don't know how to say it, it's so hard to explain . . .'

'I understand.'

He gives me an intent look, as if making sure I mean what I say, then goes on. 'And I knew at once that she was dead. It was . . .' He stops. Finally he shakes himself, literally, and goes on in his normal manner.

'And so I became a whole Leo. My only problem was that I couldn't play the tabla any more.'

I should have guessed, that restless tapping of his fingers on the table, anywhere . . .

'My mother loved music, she'd been learning it as a girl. After her marriage, it stopped. I imagine it was my grandmother who did that. And so my mother turned her ambitions on us, on my sister, rather. She was the one who sang. I accompanied her on the tabla. What's the matter? Why are you looking at me that way?'

'I was trying to imagine you a *tabalji*.' I laugh. 'No, I can't. You know, I always feel sorry for those poor men. Playing second fiddle all their lives.'

'But that's not true.' He's horrified. 'The two go together. Sometimes you can even command. Lead the singer by the nose, sort of.'

'And here I was imagining all *tabaljis* look so cynical, so

118

weary of the world because they're frustrated men. And if they're not that, they're wild, desperate men . . .'

'Like this, eh?'

He begins drumming on the table, a rapid, wild tattoo, his eyes rolling, his hair dancing about his swinging head. The waiter, after one amazed look, stands, plates in hand, politely waiting for him to finish. People at other tables stare. Bhaskar stops abruptly.

'Exactly. And do you know, I've suddenly remembered, I was learning music too once.'

'There you are! Another link between the Leos. But go on – what happened?'

'Nothing. I pestered Papa until he took me to our local nightingale one summer vacation. But she wouldn't touch shoddy amateurs. So I was returned to Papa labelled "no good".'

'Did you mind?'

'A bit. My ego was bruised. But I was relieved. After listening to her – and her daughter – I'd begun to realise I was no good.'

'Jyoti would have been good – even great, possibly.'

The food arrives and in the way I've begun to know, he turns his entire attention on it. It's only after we've served ourselves and are eating that we go back to our conversation.

'Bhaskar and Jyoti – what a good combination of names.'

'My mother chose them. She wanted names that couldn't be shortened, or twisted out of shape, she said.'

'My father was like that. I was always Urmila to him, never Urmi. My grandfather too. People's names are very important, he used to say. You shouldn't take liberties with them. It's funny, because his wife, my Baiajji, systematically took people's names away from them. Maybe because she had lost her own. I never knew her name was Kamala; everyone, even Papa, called her Bai. And she couldn't

119

remember names, either. It was always "whatshisname" or "whatshername" and one had to guess from the context. I became very clever at that.'

'And what were you to her?'

'Oh, Urmi and Bala and Sonu – anything, everything. Amrut was Ambu and Papa was Dadu, God knows why, don't ask me. Even my dignified grandfather was Aju. You know, it suddenly occurs to me, maybe that's how Amrut and I got into the habit of giving names to people.'

'Like?'

I tell him about them and like a child, waiting for a sequel in a story, he listens to me intently, giving me the right response each time. Only once, when I speak of the name Amrut and I had for Vanaa's family, he falters.

'The Coles? Why?'

I try to explain, 'Inni's superior attitude . . . *Emma* . . . Jane Austen . . .', a laboured explanation that I finally have to give up. 'So here the Leos part ways,' I laugh.

'Why? Because I've never read Jane Austen? And you do?'

'Hmm. It was with her that I began reading. And, do you know, I began because in the edition we had at home, there was a picture of Jane Austen and she looked so like my Baiajji . . .'

'Like your grandmother?'

'Yes, like this.' I plump out my cheeks and he laughs.

'When you speak of your grandmother, you look so . . . so . . .' He can't get the word.

'She brought me up.'

'But, tell me, why did your parents send you away to live with your grandparents?'

'Why?'

'You must have been a horror,' I think of Amrut saying, smoothing down his hair, preening himself. 'Look how they kept me with them.'

But that was a joke. Or, was it?

'I don't know,' I say at last. After a moment's silence he says, 'Well, never mind that. Tell me about your grandmother.'

The past is always clearer because it is more comprehended; we can grasp it as a whole. The present, maddeningly chaotic and unclear, keeps eluding us.

I realise this when he says to me, orders me rather, 'Tell me about your grandmother'. And suddenly, a swarm of memories descend on me. Like the colours that emerge from a prism, each one is real and distinct in itself, yet they are part of a whole as well – a whole, whose pattern I can see clearly.

I can see Baiajji tying her hair into a knot, skewering it with her silver pin, her face determined and earnest, her mind, I know, racing to the tasks ahead of her. I can feel the matt surface of Baiajji's books as I pass my palms over them – the fascinating smell of the old, rarely-turned pages tantalises me once again, the sharpness of their gilt edges nicks my fingertips. I get a whiff of the wet dank smell of Baiajji's garden as we go about inspecting the complicated maze of runnels that carry water from the well to all her plants. I am under the densely-leaved branches of the jamun tree, the chattering of the birds above me, the ground under my feet pocked with half-eaten jamuns, my tongue like indigo-coloured blotting paper after eating them. I can see the durbar hall during Amrut's naming ceremony, the red and white stripes in the carpet, Aju's initials in red, woven in a corner and the fragrance of flowers, attar and incense sticks wafting about me. And the durbar hall again, bare and dark, with Aju's white-shrouded body looking pathetically small on the expanse of the black and white tiled floor, Papa sitting stonily by it. I can see the blue and red *shamiana* billowing gently in and out on my wedding day, I can hear the gentle papery rustle of the leaves of the peepul tree above us, the moment of absolute silence as we wait for the guests to arrive.

Such a mélange of pictures, but nowhere can I find an answer to the question, 'Why did my parents send me away?' I'm not sure I want to find the answer, either, not here, not now anyway. So I let it alone and rummage among my memories for something to offer this man, picking and choosing with care.

And so I tell him about Baiajji and Grace Taylor, the woman who taught Baiajji English and of the books she got for Baiajji to read. I tell him of how Baiajji formally transferred the books to me when I was twelve and of how it was with them that my passion for books began. 'I have them with me still,' I tell him. I speak to him of my longing for a bike and of my joy when Papa bought me one, of the ecstasy of my first ride on it.

I relive, as I talk to him, the excitement of the day the men came to pluck the tamarinds; their cries as they clambered up the gnarled trunks, the commotion as they shook the branches, called out to one another and beat at the fruits. I experience it once again, the melancholy, the feeling of something dying, after they have gone, leaving behind them the debris of limp, dying branches, crackling shells, dark, glistening seeds and foul *bidi* stubs. I tell him of the tremendous once-a-year preparations for Baiajji's *Chaitra-Gouri haldi-kumkum*, and of how different she looked on that day, her tiny wrists encircled by heavy gold *patlis*, the pearl choker round her neck giving her a stiff, haughty look.

I tell him of the novel Amrut and I had planned to write, of the characters we invented for it: Ronald, the stern Englishman, Mabel, his washed-out wife, Sita, the dusky Indian princess with long rippling hair and Jai, the fiery revolutionary. Bhaskar laughs as I tell him of how we acted out the

122

roles, Amrut and I, Amrut, as Ronald, puffing at an imaginary pipe, and saying in a deep voice, 'By Jove' and 'God bless my soul'. While I, as poor docile Mabel, grieving over the two pathetic little graves (Robin and Sylvia – yes, even the names come back) said, 'Yes, dear' and 'Very well, dear'.

'Bored?' I ask him.

'Bored?' He offers the word back to me as if he does not know what to do with it.

And only then I come out of it and realise how intently he has been listening to me, forgetting even to eat, as if this means something to him. And it occurs to me that I have never spoken of these things to anyone, because the only people I can talk to of myself – Kishore, Amrut and Vanaa – know all this anyway. But this man . . .

Why have I retrieved my past for him? What can it mean to him? I can't go on any more. It's impossible.

'Well . . .' I say hesitantly.

'Well?' he replies questioningly. And then, after waiting for me to speak, he says 'Well,' again, with a note of finality in it this time, as if he knows I will not say anything more. Both of us know the evening is over.

After invoking my past for Bhaskar, I should have dreamt of Baiajji and my childhood; but it was Anu who came into my dream instead, Anu and Kishore. No, Anu wasn't in it, actually, it was her absence I dreamt of. I'd lost her, or rather, left her behind in a strange house, and Kishore, who came upon me as I was racing through unknown streets, desperately trying to find my way back to Anu, refused to take me to her. He drove on, deaf to my frantic pleas. At which point I woke up, my mind still a riot of confused feelings, Kishore's disembodied voice lingering in my ears. And the whole day I have been left with an uneasy sense of something undone, something I should have done for Anu, but hadn't. What was it?

I wanted so much for Anu; now, it's all gone, there's nothing left of all my hopes for her. We dream so much more for our daughters than we do for our sons, we want to give them the world we dreamt of for ourselves. 'I wanted Kalpana to have all that I didn't,' Shakutai told me. But Kalpana wanted none of her mother's dreams. She had her own. Mira too:

> To make myself in your image
> was never the goal I sought.

Do we always turn our backs on our mother's hopes? I have often had twinges of regret for thwarting Papa when I forswore ambition and turned away from anything that meant competing. But now I realise Inni had her dreams for me too. She saw me vaulting out of the middle-class with marriage, making the kind of marriage that would let me live the life that was her ideal, a 'pearls and chiffons' sort of existence, Amrut and I called it. Instead, I married the boy-next-door, 'Whose father,' Inni sobbed out, 'eats *paan*, and whose mother is a school teacher'. I had laughed then at the pettiness of Inni's objections, but does that make her pain less real?

And Anu . . .? Would she have felt the same? I will let her soar, I had thought, I will let nothing fetter her, not even my love. She will go far, she will climb high, she will do anything she wants. Would she have rejected this, laughed at me and burdened herself with 'silver toe-rings and tinkling anklets'?

> Green sari draped about me
> green bangles encircle my wrists,
> fill your eyes with the sight, mother,
> look at me, fruitful and green.

Silver toe-rings twinkle on my toes
silver anklets tinkle as I walk
but, oh mother, I stumble, I fall
my arms sink heavily by my sides.

'Woman's vision' . . . It was Priti who used the words to
me. 'I want your vision, a woman's vision' she said and I
had laughed at her. I thought it ridiculous that two persons
should share a vision only because they belong to the same
sex. Vanaa and I now, we grew up together, on two sides
of a hedge; but our visions are as different as the views our
houses, facing opposite directions, had. Yet I can remember
the vague sense of discomfort that came over me when I
watched a scene in an old movie, a scene of haunting
beauty, in which Waheeda, singing a song as she gets ready
to meet a lover, smiles at her reflection while she draws a
kaajal-lined finger across her eyelids. It seemed too narcis-
sistic, the woman's admiration of herself. Now I realise –
this was not a woman looking at herself. It was a man
looking at a woman, this was how a man saw a woman. A
man's vision.

And now Mira's poem. I read it and can see her standing
before her mother in her green sari and green bangles; I
can imagine how it was for her, the fluttering, fearful sense
of having life within her. And, strangely enough, I can
connect myself to her mother as well, for it was I who, as
the daughter-in-law of the family, performed this ritual for
Vanaa before Mandira was born, with Akka directing me,
telling me what I had to do. When it was all done and Vanaa
clumsily got up, her sari end burdened with the ritual grains
and coconut, held before her, there was a moment's
confusion, even Akka uncertain for the first time. If it was
Akka who had done all this, Vanaa would have bent down
and touched her feet; but I . . .? We looked at each other
and Vanaa suddenly ended the moment by laughing. She

125

hugged me and I could feel her body, huge, ungainly, pulsating with life, I could see her face alight with happiness.

But Mira was not joyful. At least her poem isn't. What was it that weighed her down? Was it the fact that she was bearing the child of a man she did not love? Mira lost this child, anyway. And when she found herself with child again, her mother was dead.

My mother is dead. She died happy, they tell me. She saw me married, she saw me pregnant and she was happy. I am supposed to comfort myself with this thought. But I can find no comfort in it, not for myself, anyway. She is dead, that is the truth. What does it matter whether she died happy or unhappy? Yet I am glad I told her nothing. What if I had? What could she have done? Nothing. That was all she could do in her entire life – nothing. 'Don't ask me,' she used to say to us. 'Nothing is in my hands.' She knew I was not happy, I know she knew it; but she was afraid to ask me, afraid I would admit it. No, I am glad I never told her anything.

They all think I am grieving because I could not meet her before she died. Am I? Yes, I am. But there is more. I wish I could have asked her a question. 'Mother,' I always wanted to ask, 'Why do you want me to repeat your history when you so despair of your own?' But she died and I will never know her answer now.

There is no answer in this poem, either. Only a fear, that you can never escape.

Whose face is this I see in the mirror,
unsmiling, grave, bedewed with fear?
The daughter? No, Mother, I am now your shadow.

Mira was only 22 when she wrote this. She had been married at the age of 18. Since then, she had lived a life which, even if normal to most women of that time, must have seemed terrible to her. It seems appalling to me when I think of the choices of my own life, of its freedom. Cloistered in a home, living with a man she could not love, surrounded by people she had nothing in common with – how did she go on?

Perhaps it was her writing that kept her going, that kept her alive. When and where did she write? Certainly she could never have had, in that house, a room of her own. Except at night. Yes, I imagine it was there that she wrote, late at night, after the man had gone to bed. I can see her stealthily, soundlessly getting out of bed, sitting down on the floor by the window perhaps, forgetting everything while she wrote. Did she think of Venu then? Did she remember his words 'I am only an instrument' and how proudly he said that? Did she remember how she had told herself she would write like him one day? Did she remember the young boys and girls thronging around him, lionising him?

She met him once. She does not say where or when, but she writes in her diary of the meeting. Perhaps she spoke to him of her poetry – I can imagine it was a desperate kind of courage that made her speak of it – gave him some of her poems to read. And he said, yes, she has written this, quoted his actual words: 'Why do you need to write poetry? It is enough for a young woman like you to give birth to children. That is your poetry. Leave the other poetry to us men.'

Venu . . . even I knew his name. Papa was an admirer of his. 'He's that rare thing, a born poet,' Papa used to say. I remember Papa uncharacteristically tongue-tied when he met him once at a function, and, like a schoolboy, held out a copy of his book for Venu to autograph. I was there too

127

at that function, in the last year of Venu's life, when he was honoured. I can remember the frail, bewildered figure and his wife, anxious and watchful by him, the admirers who surrounded him. He died just a year later, a grand old man of Indian literature, one of the great poets of the century, having won all the awards and honours that there are. Now he is a cult figure, his poems everywhere, sung on the radio, TV, even in films.

And Mira . . .? The tapping on the wall is finally beginning to make sense. Something comes through when I think of Venu's poems everywhere and Mira's voice silenced.

They are sitting on the bed, clothes strewn about them. For an instant I think it is Inni's Delhi shopping being displayed; then I realise the clothes are mine.

'What's going on?'

They look up, eyes blank and unfocused and go back to the clothes without replying.

'Look at this, Vanaa. I always wondered why this sari looks so dull when Urmi wears it. Now I know. She wears it with a white blouse – imagine that! What she needs is a blouse this shade . . .'

Inni's pink-tinted nail points to a spot on my sari. Throwing my bag on a chair, I repeat my question. They continue to ignore me.

'You're right. You know, Inniauntie, you could earn quite a good living as a . . .'

'Will you tell me what you're doing?'

'Really, Urmi, you're the limit! Not one of your cottons is starched.'

'I hate my clothes standing away from me, as if they're disowning me. I like them to be part of me.'

'Don't talk pretentious nonsense. And look at these sleeves . . . why don't you make sleeves all the way down to your wrists and have done with it?'

128

'Because I don't want to look like Mrs Gandhi on an election campaign.'

'Mrs G.? You couldn't do better than try to look like her. That woman was chic.'

'Chic!'

'Stop quarrelling. And Urmi, come and sit down for Heaven's sake. I'm doing this for you.'

'What are you doing?'

'Trying to make a well-dressed female out of you.'

'I am well dressed.'

'Well dressed! Not one sari with a matching blouse.'

'I think it's a waste of time going from shop to shop "matching".'

Inni's forgotten me again. 'Look at this, Vanaa, isn't it a lovely shade? I have a sari exactly this colour, it'll go beautifully with this. I think I'll give it to Urmi.'

'Inni, please . . .'

But Inni, looking flushed and energetic, is already out of the room. Vanaa grins. 'Where's Amrut? Inniauntie said you were lunching together.'

'On his way. He stopped at the chemist's. Here, Vanaa, clear this up, I want to lie down.'

'They're your clothes. You clear up.'

'Don't be cheeky.'

'Look, this one.' Inni holds out her sari, as always impeccably ironed and on a hanger. 'Get up, Urmi, I want to see how this looks on you.'

There's no arguing with Inni in this mood. I obediently stand up while she drapes the sari over my left shoulder and steps back to gaze reflectively at me.

'I knew it would look good on her. Stand straight, Urmi. And don't be so stiff. See, Vanaa? I knew it would suit her complexion. One thing about Urmi, any colour suits her. If only she would learn to dress better. She learnt this

129

shabbiness from her grandmother . . . Stand still, Urmi, don't move.'

Her hands shove and pull me about roughly, her voice is sharp and she seems scarcely aware of me as a person; but I can feel her love. Look, she seems to be saying in wonder, look, this is my daughter. And in an instant the full extent of my loss comes over me. I've lost not just my baby Anu as a child, as a girl, as a young woman . . . I feel breathless, aghast with the weight of my loss.

'Are you listening to me, Urmi?'

'Yes, you've been abusing my poor Baiajji. Leave her alone.'

'I wasn't saying anything about your precious Baiajji. I was just telling you to do something about these clothes.'

'You're right. I shall bundle them back into the cupboard, I've had enough of them.'

Inni realises my mood has changed. 'Where's Amrut?' she asks, shelving the topic of clothes.

'He's coming.' The bell rings. 'There, that must be him.' I push the clothes aside and lie down.

'Urmi, don't. Put those clothes away first.'

'You took them out, you put them back. Oh, all right, if you're so stubborn . . .'

Amrut comes in and stretches himself on the bed.

'Amrut, don't . . .'

'Don't what?'

'How was the celebration?'

'What celebration?'

'Amrut, get up.'

'Inniauntie said you'd gone out to celebrate your success. How was it?'

'Riotous. Didi paid, so I . . .'

'Amrut, get off those clothes!'

'What? Oh, these. You could have told me gently. No need to yell.' He pulls them out from under him and hands

130

them to me, crushed into a bundle, with a reproving look. 'Do you have to be so messy, Didi? Here, fold them and put them away.'

'God give me patience.'

'Temper, big sister, temper. What's wrong with her?'

'Nothing. Just being her usual sunny self. But Inniauntie's making up. She's in a wonderful mood.'

'Naturally. With her beloved son one step closer to the haloed IAS.'

'I can almost see her dreams ballooning about her head.'

'Poor Inni. Even if I get through the viva, I'm going to be just a lowly menial for the next few years. Like those kids who crawl about your feet cleaning the floor in restaurants. Can I lie down now?'

'Tired, eh?'

Amrut groans loudly and dramatically.

'Poor Amrut.' Vanaa clicks her tongue. 'Looking forward to getting back to Delhi?'

'You bet. I'm a sensitive sort. Your Bombay makes me nervous.'

'Bombay's real, child,' I retort, banging the door of my cupboard. 'Delhi is just so much hot air, inflated with its idea of itself.'

'Anyone want tea?' Inni calls out. 'I'm making a cup for Amrut.'

'Yes, Inni, I do.'

'Me too, Inniauntie. Gosh, Amrut, you are being favoured. Inniauntie herself making tea for you!'

'What do you think?' Amrut smirks in mock complacency, then suddenly subsides into gloom. 'But I'm sure I'm going to fail next time. I don't know what gives me the feeling, I just know.'

'I don't see you doing that; not with Radha behind you.'

'The woman behind the successful man, eh?'

'Stop it, Urmi.' Amrut takes off his glasses, gives them

131

to me to put away and turns over, his face pressed into the pillow.

'And can you believe it, Vanaa, he doesn't intend telling Inni about Radha.'

'What's there to tell?' Amrut mumbles.

'Don't be dishonest. Inni's on the prowl, I'm warning you. She told me about her friend Malini's daughter . . .'

'And someone's niece . . .'

'All "Nice, our type, Maharashtrian girls". Instead, poor Inni, she's going to get a Tamil girl . . .'

'Ssssshhhhh.'

'Poor Amrut, don't be scared, we won't tell. But you must tell Inniauntie yourself.'

'Leave the poor boy alone, Vanaa. He'll do that when Radha delivers her ultimatum. Or her mother does.'

'Formidable female, is she?'

'Uh hunh.'

'Poor Amrut. But don't worry, Amrut, if she tries to start something, call us.'

'Come on, Vanaa, come off it. I thought you were a kind woman, unlike this big sister of mine.'

'The good old British policy of divide and rule. But we will not fall for it.'

'No, we stand together . . .'

Inni comes in with the tea and Amrut springs up, crying 'Ah, tea'. He goes back to his clowning self, but I can see he is really displeased and hurt by our jokes.

'I'm sorry, Ambu,' I say to him later, 'I'm sorry if we hurt your feelings.'

'And so you should be.'

'I never thought you'd mind a bit of funning.'

'Funning? No, it's more than that. Tell me, Didi, do you females admire only the men who crush you? Do you despise men who don't?'

'I suppose you're asking me if I despise you because

132

you're soft. The answers are, firstly, I don't despise you, and secondly, I don't think you're soft.'

'Yes, but I'm asking you a general question.'

'In general? Well, I don't know about others, I can only speak for myself and the answer is . . . What is the answer? Let me think. No, I don't like men who try to dominate women. I don't like women who do it to men, either. But yes, a man must be firm. Like Papa was . . .'

'Papa was dominating. There's no other word for him. Things were simple to him, "You have to do things my way", and that was it.'

'I never found him so rigid!'

'How often and how long did you live in his house? I did. He was absolute master in his house. I felt sorry for poor Inni.'

'Poor Inni, my foot! Inni wantd Papa to be master. She'd have hated it any other way.'

'There! That answers my question. Women do want to be dominated.'

'You can't generalise that way, Amrut. It's just that Inni was weak – well, the weaker of the two.'

'And so it's fine if Papa dominates her. But, if between Radha and me, I'm weaker . . .'

'You're not, I know you, you just hate conflict . . .'

'And she dominates, it makes me ridiculous and her hateful. Why is that, Didi? Tell me. I always thought Papa was brutal.'

'No, Amrut, that's too harsh!'

'Why? Do you think you have to use physical violence to be brutal? Even to force your will on another is to be brutal. Why are you looking at me that way?'

'Out of the mouths of babes and sucklings . . . Oh, sorry, Amrut, I'm really sorry. Anyway, I think you should tell Inni . . .'

'When the time comes, when the time comes,' he says

airily. 'You remember how you rushed into telling Papa about you and Kishore and what a fine furore there was – Papa furious, Inni crying. I was your only support, remember?'

'Some support! I fought my battle alone.'

'Fought my battle alone! You make it sound terribly romantic – the world against the lovers – Hindi-fillum style. But Papa gave in soon enough, didn't he?'

I laugh.

'What's the joke?'

'Papa gave in . . . Do you know how he did it? He quoted a line to me. *Sokamayata bahusyam prajayeya iti* . . .'

'What does that mean?'

'That's what I asked him. And he explained, with a scornful smile on his face – you know how he used to look. It's from the *Upanisads*, he said. It means, every living cell desires to multiply. And so, he said, I know I can't stop you. That put me in my place. Merely a living cell, wanting to multiply.'

'Yeah, that's Papa all right.'

'Anyway, Amrut, in spite of all that you didn't do for me, I'll support you when you tell Inni about Radha. She's a nice girl.'

'Who? Inni?'

'Idiot!'

Amrut has gone. We have parted, as always, friends. I miss him, the house seems dull and quiet without him; but the routine of daily life is a giant sponge that absorbs everything. Except pain. And boredom. Inni feels his absence the most. Her face reminds me of Baiajji's when Papa, Inni and Amrut left Ranidurg. 'The house is ready to eat us up, isn't it, Bala?' she used to ask me dolefully. Was that why she had that elaborate ceremonial leave-taking ritual? Maybe it helped to take the edge off the sharpness of

134

feeling. It amazes me when I think of it now, all the fuss that Baiajji made – the special meal in the morning, with *khir* and tiny frill-edged *karanjis*, the preparations in the *puja* room in the afternoon, my job being to prime the oil lamps with oil-soaked wicks, while Baiajji drew the *rangoli*. And just when you thought all the formalities were over, Baiajji would rush out with the curds for the travellers, a thick sliver trembling on the flat of the palm, to be licked off, 'So that you come back soon'.

And there is Kishore, who walks away as if he's going down for an after-dinner stroll. He allows no farewells; not even Inni is permitted to make a thing out of it.

'You're lucky,' Inni says to me each time he's gone, 'you don't feel things like I do.'

'Yes, Inni, I'm lucky,' I agree. I'd rather leave her innocence unsmeared, never let her know of the anger and grief that fills me, so painful it is as if I'm being pierced by multitudes of sharp knives.

Now, with Amrut gone, there's just a sense of emptiness and dullness. Worse this time, because I've come to the end of Mira's poems. This has been like a parting too. And yet it is no parting, because Mira in some strange way stays with me, I know she will never go. All these days I have been imagining myself the hunter and Mira my prey; I have been filled with the excitement of the hunter each time I approached her. Suddenly our relationship has changed. It is Mira who is now taking me by the hand and leading me . . . Where? I don't know, I have no idea what lies at the end of this remarkable journey, but on the way I have seen Kishore.

So often, since I came upon Mira, I have looked for a resemblance between Kishore and his mother. I have searched for it in the eyes, the expression, the smile. Now I realise it's been staring me in the face ever since I began reading Mira. It's here, in her poem about her unborn child.

135

This is her last poem. I'm sure it is, because it is the only one that's complete, yet just scribbled on a piece of paper, as if she did it in a hurry, hoping to redo it later, perhaps, to copy it out neatly like she did the others. But she never did. She died a few months later, having bled to death within an hour after her child was born. We would never have known of it if Kishore's aunt, a ghoul who loved to give people the horrors, hadn't told Vanaa the story just before Mandira was born. 'There was not a drop of blood in her body,' she had told us dramatically. 'She turned black. They kept her body till my brother went there, but he refused to look at it.' I remember Vanaa asking Akka, 'Will you look after my child if I die?' and Akka's rage when she learnt what her aunt had done.

'Women don't die in childbirth now,' she had said brusquely. But Mira did.

She wrote nothing after this poem. She lapsed into silence. I like to think that it is because she was happy, I like to think that these last months of her life were, well, if not happy, at least tranquil. That it was a period of peace for her and she was content to live each day as it came, to feel the child grow within her.

Tiny fish swimming in the ocean of my womb
my body thrills to you;
churning the ocean, shaking distant shores
you will emerge one day.

Lightning flashed through the front door
and I who was stone quivered.
Bridging the two worlds, you awaken in me
a desire for life.

Desire, says the Buddha, is the cause of grief;
but how escape this cord

136

this binding vine of love? Fear lies coiled within
this womb-piercing joy.

Smiling and joyful, Karna tore off his armour,
his body trailed blood.
Will that courage be mine when, denuded,
I stand naked and bare?

'Just one word,' Inni says when she is doing her cross-word, 'if I can get one word, the rest will follow.'

I know the feeling. When I read this poem, I feel I have found the word which will help me to solve the rest of the crossword. After Aju's death, Papa and I cleared out our Ranidurg house. When it was over, Papa, who had been as ruthless as I was in this clearing-up, looked sorrowful and bereft. But for me, there was relief. With the house cleared of everything, it was possible for me to leave it behind and go on. Now, with this poem, Mira has cleared my emotional life, swept away the confusing tangle of cobwebs.

'Do women want to be dominated?' Amrut asked me. No, Amrut, no human being wants to be dominated. The most important need is to love. From the moment of our births, we struggle to find something with which we can anchor ourselves to this strange world we find ourselves in. Only when we love do we find this anchor. But love makes you vulnerable. Mira realised this; and she was afraid. Was it this same fear I saw on Kishore's face on our wedding night?

'The two of us in a closed room,' he said, parodying the words of a popular film-song, 'and we can't get out. That's marriage.'

And I walked out, not just to prove him wrong, though there was that too, but because of the look on his face. It frightened me. He looked trapped. Sometimes I wonder whether Papa had seen this look, whether that was why he had tried to dissuade me from marrying Kishore. Yet that night, when I went back home, Papa asked me no questions. It was Amrut who came to my room and, with an anxiety he tried to conceal, called out 'All right, Didi?'

'Yes,' I said and fell asleep in the midst of all the chaos in my room. When I woke up the next morning, Kishore was having tea with the family. He must have walked through the hedge as casually as he had done all through the years. He did not speak of my having walked out at night; nor did I. When I had my tea, we got up to go back to his home. As we were leaving, I remember it now, Inni broke down. Inni, who had been silent until then, clung to me and cried, making desolate, sniffling little sounds. Papa gently detached her from me and I wiped her face. And Kishore, I can remember this too, and so distinctly, watched us, that remote look on his face again.

'Each time you leave me, the parting is like death.'

The words came to my mind the first time he left me to go back to his ship. I did not say them aloud. Perhaps, I knew even then I could never say the words to him. I never have.

But that evening, I thought I would die if I didn't speak.

'Missing the brats?' Kishore asked, looking into my face.

'No.'

'Good. Tomorrow we're back with them. Let's make the most of our last evening by ourselves.'

I felt a kind of superstitious dread when he said 'last evening' but pushed it away and went to get dressed.

Nothing is ever lost or forgotten. I thought I'd put this evening away on a high shelf, I didn't want to recollect it; but now, at this touch of a probing finger, memories cascade down on me. I can see myself standing before Kishore, smoothing the rich silk of my sari. Baiajji's old sari. Rust-coloured silk. And the gold in the border glowing. And Kishore saying, 'My God, Urmi, you're beautiful!'

138

And I, laughing, saying, 'I thought it was understood that Inni is the beauty of the family. I'm not.'

'Not always. Only in flashes. But God, Urmi, what flashes!' And he kissed me on the lips.

It was that kind of an evening. I felt drunk with his admiration. I can see the two of us at the dining table, I can hear myself laughing, I can hear the tinkle as one of my pins fell into my plate.

'Such elegant dishevelment,' Kishore said, holding my hair loosely bunched in his hand, and at the touch of his fingers on the nape of my neck, I shivered. As we walked back along the beach, we heard the distant rumble of thunder. We did not hurry and the rain, colluding with us, held off until we had got into our room.

Then it began, in a startling burst of fury, battering at the door, the windows, drumming on the roof. The lights went out. I lit a candle and stood before the mirror, plaiting my hair. I could see Kishore in the mirror; was it a trick of the candlelight, or some fault in the ancient mirror that made him look so distant? Suddenly I thought, 'I will say it to him now, I will tell him how I feel.'

It was like a fantasy. I saw myself crying out to him, 'Don't leave me and go. Each time you leave me, the parting is like death.' I saw myself stretching out my arms to him, putting them round his neck – the classic, clinging female. And the fantasy relentlessly went on: I saw him detach himself from me, distaste on his face, I heard him . . .

'Come on, Narcissus, come to bed. Haven't you had enough of your reflection?'

There was this, anyway. He stroked my eyebrows, traced the outline of my ear, murmured my name endlessly into it. He traced my lips with his fingers, his tongue, he set my body on fire with his hands. The rain, the thunder receded.

But sex is only a temporary answer. I came out of it to

find that the lights had come back. Kishore lay smoking, one arm under his head, his face clear and calm in the pool of light the bed-lamp threw over it. I lay still and watched an insect crawl on the edge of the lampshade, casting a Kafkaesque shadow on the wall. It teetered, almost fell off, clung on again, wobbled and finally dropped down. Kishore leaned across and stubbed his cigarette butt into the ashtray. It was the finality of the gesture that shattered my strange inertia. I got out of bed, pulled on my nightdress.

'Where are you going?'

'Out.'

'Have you gone crazy?'

I opened the door and stepped out into a roar of sound. The wind and the rain buffeted at my face, the drops hammered on my skull. I heard Kishore calling to me, but I walked on. I was soaked in a moment, my nightdress clung to me, I could not walk, I began hobbling. 'Urmi,' he shouted into my ear as if I was deaf. Suddenly I sagged. He put his arm round me and led me back to our room. 'Have a bath,' he said and when I came out, a towel wrapped man-like about my waist, I saw he had made the bed. It was smooth and unwrinkled, all traces of our lovemaking wiped out.

'Go to sleep,' he said. He was kneeling by me, his face close to mine, but the closeness was only physical. His voice was cold. I could see the goose bumps on his shoulders, his chest. I did not look into his face, I was afraid of what I would see. I turned round and fell asleep. And woke up only when he shook me awake and said, 'We have to go back, Anu is not well.'

> *Desire, says the Buddha, is the cause of grief;*
> *but how escape this cord*
> *this binding vine of love? Fear lies coiled within*
> *this womb-piercing joy.*

Yes, here it is, the knowledge I spared myself then. Kishore will never remove his armour, there is something in him I will never reach. I have lived with the hope that some day I will. Each relationship, always imperfect, survives on hope. Am I to give up this hope? Is this what Mira is offering me?

Everything here seems unchanged as if it has been fossilised: the flour mill with its snaky row of tins; the child before the grocer's shop, standing on her toes, tapping with a coin on the lid of a glass jar to draw the man's attention; the children playing cricket against the wall. Only the movie posters on the wall have been changed; but it makes no difference, for there is still a woman with an enormous bust forcing itself through a skimpy blouse, a man with a gun, his face twisted into a kind of exaggerated macho rage. I enter the central common courtyard and find a small group watching two men replacing some tiles on the roof. Sandhya is one of them. Perhaps she senses my presence for she turns round, sees me, and calling out 'auntie' runs towards me. Suddenly she stops, swivels round and races off towards their room. When I get there she is frantically tidying up, flinging things into their places, trying to make room for me to sit down on the bed.

'Is your mother at home, Sandhya?'

'Yes, auntie, come in, I'll call her.'

'Isn't she well?'

'No, auntie, she's all right today, sit here, auntie . . .' She pats a spot and watches anxiously until I sit down. 'I'll call her.' She goes out, yells 'Ai-ga' and returns.

'What was wrong with her?'

'She had fever. There she is . . . Ai . . .'

Shakutai comes in, wiping her hands on her sari. Panic flows into her face when she sees me.

'Urmila . . .? Is Kalpana . . .?'

'She's all right. I came to see you. The nurse said you hadn't been to the hospital for two days.'

'A little fever. I get it once a year. I'm all right now. I sent Prakash to the hospital yesterday. Today he refused to go. You'll have some tea?'

'No, don't bother.'

'Why is it a bother? You've come so far, you must have something. Sandhya . . .'

But Sandhya is already in the corner by the stove.

'No school for Sandhya today?'

'I didn't send her. If she goes, who'll do the work here?'

'Sulumavshi said . . .'

'Yes, yes, let Sulumavshi clean your vessels, wash your clothes, let her do all your dirty work. This child has no sense.'

While Sandhya makes the tea, we talk. The thundering of the trains on the railway lines just behind the house provides a backdrop to our conversation. It seems to me there's something hostile about these trains. I have a sense of panic when one approaches, my heart starts hammering as if echoing the sound. The building shakes, vessels rattle. But the woman, to whom the sound is a part of her life, goes on talking, raising her voice each time a train approaches, dropping it to its normal level the instant the sounds die away.

Shakutai's obsession with Kalpana has made her neglectful of the others, of her home. I can see the neglect, like a slight overlay of dust, over the room, over the child herself, who, after getting us the tea, sits listening to us, her arms round her knees, her eyes fixed on my face, as if she is trying to memorise my features. It makes me uneasy. I am relieved when she gets up as soon as a cat stalks in.

'Shoo, shoo,' the mother says, but Sandhya protests.

'It's come for its milk, Ai.' She gets some in a saucer and kneels by it, chirruping to it, dropping her head as the level

142

of the milk goes down, until she is almost face to face with the cat.

'You and your cat, wasting milk on it,' Shakutai says, but without rancour.

'It's not mine, it's Kalpana's.'

'Kalpana – all she did was feed it for a few days! And that because I told her we couldn't afford to give milk to an animal.'

'But you let her keep it.'

'What could I do? Sulu told me, "Don't say 'no' to her for everything".' She turns to me. 'I don't want to deprive the children of anything. I even bought them a TV set. Why should my children go to other people's houses to watch? Are they beggars? I've deprived them of nothing,' she repeats. 'And Kalpana . . . Sandhya, get that box.'

Sandhya, stroking the cat, asks, 'What box?'

'Kalpana's. Here, look at this,' she says, opening the old biscuit tin Sandhya brings, 'have you ever seen such a collection of rubbish?'

The box is full of a variety of hair clips, bands, bangles . . .

'And you should see the bottles – bottles of nail paint. What do you need to paint your nails for? I asked her. The first thing she did was to buy herself a mirror. She was forever looking at herself in the mirror. Trash!' she says bitterly, banging the tin shut.

'It's not trash, Ai, look, this is beautiful.' Sandhya opens the tin again and picks out a pair of butterflies in colour.

'Take it, wear it then.'

'Kalpana will be angry with me.'

'Where is she to get angry with you? You're quite safe. Wear it, wear it.'

The girl, with a doubtful look on her face, fixes the pins in her hair. Then she touches them as if to make sure they're there. There is a beatific smile on her face. Every

143

now and then her hands go to the slides, feeling them, reassuring herself they're there.

'Sometimes I think she'll never come home any more. We've lost her. She will die, Urmila, she will die.'

Shakutai begins to cry. Sandhya comes closer to her and repeats helplessly, 'Ai, don't cry, don't cry.' The woman goes on with her keening. After a while she quietens down; I can see the effort behind it.

'Sandhya, go and get the flour from the mill, child. I left the wheat there in the morning, it must be floured by now, get it.'

'Later, Ai.'

'No, I need it for the evening, I can't make chapatties otherwise.'

When the girl has reluctantly gone, she begins to cry again, her voice hoarse, her sobs stifled in her sari.

'Shakutai, don't. This does no good, what's the use of it?'

She calms herself with an effort again.

'It seems to me I came into this world carrying a load of misfortunes. I thought my Sulu was lucky. I thought, when she married Prabhakar, she at least would have a good life. He's a good man, he doesn't touch drink, not even cigarettes . . . Yes, I thought her luck is great. But who knows what is hidden in our fate?' She says, after a pause, 'God has given her no children.' Suddenly so many things are clear – the tenderness in her voice when she speaks of Sulu, the pity that runs like a refrain through all her talk of her sister.

'And do you know, he hasn't said an angry word to her about it – not once. Any other man would have given his wife hell. But Prabhakar . . . And Sulu knows her luck. Whatever he wants is done at once.'

A boy runs in, calling out, 'Ai, Ai . . .' in a hoarse,

144

peremptory voice. He stops suddenly on seeing me, his face goes blank. Then he turns round and goes out.

'Prakash, Prakash . . .'

Sandhya comes in, the tin of flour balanced on her skinny hip, her face transformed by the fine dusting of flour on her hair. It looks a startling, incongruous grey above the child's face.

'He's gone. Shall I call him back, Ai?'

'No, never mind, he'll come himself. Sandhya, where's the album?'

'The one Sulumavshi gave us?'

'Yes, where is it? Get it, I want to show Urmila Kalpana's photos.'

She wipes the album tenderly with her sari end before opening it. The child sits by us, all animation now, looking at the pictures as if she's never seen them before. There aren't many of them.

'Look, this is my Sulu and her husband.'

It's a wedding photograph. They are posed in the manner of all newly-wed couples, the girl moon-faced, all expression blanked out, the man square-jawed, looking sternly into the camera.

'And this one – we took it when Kalpana was born. Sulu is the one who insisted . . .'

The mother and daughter exclaim and chatter over each photograph, I make the appropriate comments.

'Here's Kalpana and Madhuri – she's her great friend, they worked in the shop together – they went and got themselves photographed, just two or three months back. Kalpana was dressed up, lipstick and all, when I came home that day. When I asked her where she was going, she wouldn't tell me. It was Madhuri who said "We're going to the studio to have our photograph taken." "Wipe off that lipstick," I told Kalpana, but she didn't even reply. Just walked off . . .'

145

I am suddenly full of pity for Kalpana. I imagine her, like Sandhya with the slides, passing her tongue over her lips, making sure the lipstick is there, convincing herself of her adulthood.

'What's wrong with lipstick, Shakutai?'

'You don't understand, Urmila, it's not only the lipstick. Here boys are like . . . they're like dogs panting after bitches. And if you paint and flaunt yourself, do you think they'll leave you alone? Ever since Kalpana grew up, I have had to live with this fear. But Kalpana doesn't understand. Once she started earning, she thought she could do what she wanted.'

'Look, Ai, she tried to tear up this one . . .'

Shakutai looks at the photograph for a moment in silence, then passes it to me.

'She was wearing her first sari. I bought Sulu her first sari and Sulu said, "When Kalpu grows up, Shakutai, I'll buy her her first sari." She did. And Kalpana refused to wear it. You know girls these days, they don't want to wear saris. But I made her wear it and Sulu took her home and they went to have this picture taken, the three of them – Sulu, Prabhakar and Kalpana. And when Sulu gave us this copy, Kalpana tried to tear it up. I don't understand that girl, Urmila, what does she want, what does she want?'

It's a cry of such rage and despair, it startles me.

'I asked her, again and again I asked her, what do you want? But she never gave me a reply.'

To you who are satiated, content
how do I speak of my wants?

But that was Mira . . .

'Put this away, Sandhya, put it away. And go and see where Prakash has gone. Tell him I want him.'

She waits until the girl has gone out before continuing.

146

'You know, Urmila, since that night when we waited for Kalpana – all night we waited – and she didn't come home, I'm afraid for my children. And I'm worried to death about Prakash.'

'What's the matter with him?'

'I don't know. He's become moody. I don't know what he's doing in school. God knows whether he's studying or not.'

'Why don't you speak to him?'

'He won't speak to me. I asked Prabhakar to talk to him, I had to, I have no man at home, whom do I turn to? He was impertinent and Prabhakar gave one or two slaps – what's wrong with that? He's like his father. But Kalpana went mad. How dare he lay his hands on Prakash, she screamed. My children have become a burden to me, Urmila, they have become a burden.' She stops, exhausted. 'And now, Prakash . . . "You should have controlled her," he says. "You let her get out of hand." I don't blame him, he listens to others. I know what they're saying. What can you expect, they say, of a girl whose mother has left her husband? Imagine! He left me for another woman, left me with these children to bring up. And I have to listen to such words because of this girl. She's shamed us, we can never wipe off this blot. And Prakash blames me. What could I do? She was so self-willed. Cover yourself decently, I kept telling her, men are like animals. But she went her way. You should have seen her walking out, head in the air, caring for nobody. It's all her fault, Urmila, all her fault . . .'

'Shakutai, for God's sake, stop this, stop blaming her. Why do you blame her, how is it her fault?'

She looks at me in amazement. 'Whose is it then? We're all disgraced because of her.'

'She was hurt, she was injured, wronged by a man; she didn't do anything wrong. Why can't you see that? Are you blind? It's not her fault, no, not her fault at all.'

147

Sandhya comes running in at the sound of our raised voices and stands staring at us with large frightened eyes.

'Whose fault is it then? Whom do I blame?'

'The man, the man who did this to her. Don't you see, can't you see he's the wrongdoer?'

She looks at me in silence, eyes wide and startled, as if the thought of the man has never occurred to her.

'The man,' she says after a small silence. 'What use is it blaming him? Women like you will never understand what it is like for us. We have to keep to our places, we can never step out. There are always people waiting to throw stones at us, our own people first of all. I warned Kalpana, but she would never listen to me. "I'm not afraid of anyone," she used to say. That's why this happened to her . . . women must know fear.'

Suddenly it is no longer possible just to listen, to make soothing sounds, to be sympathetic. I find myself rampant with anger. The woman does not seem to be able to grasp the enormity of this thing that has happened to her daughter. She goes back to the past and speaks of her daughter as a stubborn child she could not bend to her will. 'What does she want?' she asks over and over again. Sometimes she seems to forget that her daughter is unconscious and dying, and speaks as if getting raped is merely one more of those childish misdemeanours that so annoyed her. She grieves too, as often as she is angry. But through all this there is one constant strand; she talks as if the girl is to blame for what has happened to her. It's her fault, she says. She was stubborn, she was self-willed, she dressed up, she painted her lips and nails and so this happened to her. 'You should have seen her walking out, head erect, caring for nobody.'

Caring for nobody? No, that's not true. Kalpana was – is – young, at an age when her existence is still a miracle to her. And therefore she walked out of that ramshackle building with gaily painted nails and lips, brightly coloured clothes and sleek, shining hair, loudly proclaiming the miracle of that existence. All young people do it. But Kalpana was raped and her mother says it happened because she flaunted herself.

Does she really believe this? Or is she saying it to shake off the burden of guilt all parents bear? And what does she mean when she says a woman must know fear? Kalpana was not afraid, she says, and that is why this happened to her.

I don't believe, I can't believe Kalpana was not afraid. If she said she was not, it was sheer bravado. I know how fearfully I look back, my heart thudding in panic, when I hear footsteps behind me on a dark deserted street. And there is that dream of mine, a recurring nightmare of a strange man standing in the shadows at the edge of a grove of trees, who somehow so menaces me that fear enters into me. It begins right here, in the centre of my body and spreads until my entire body is filled with what I so bravely disavow in my waking hours. And I wake up drenched in sweat.

You don't understand, Shakutai said to me. But how can I not understand when the warning signposts are all about me? It is different for you, Shakutai said. But it is not. I was only a child when a boy, crazed by his adolescent desires, accosted me on a lonely path in Ranidurg. 'Come with me,' he said and, in spite of my ignorance, the look on his face terrified me. It is the same look I see mirrored on the face of a colleague; when he looks at me, even in the midst of a crowd, I feel sexually threatened.

> I feel the quickening in my womb,
> he moves – why do I call the child he?

'Why do I call the child he?' Yes, Mira, why? Why did you want a son? Is it because you were frightened of bearing this constant burden of fear for your daughter as well?

'I told her to be careful,' Shakutai moans. 'Don't go anywhere with strangers,' Vanaa cautions her daughters. 'Why are you so late?' Inni asks me accusingly if I am a little delayed. I can remember the hysteria with which she greeted me when I came home once unusually late. 'Why does God give us daughters?' Shakutai cried out and I was enraged, but it follows, yes, it follows.

Kartik stirs in his sleep. His legs are, as always, entangled in his blanket. I unwind it and cover him once again. Looking at him, my anger falters. Suddenly weary, I lay my head on the bed beside Kartik and am overcome by such a wave of longing for my daughter, it is all I can do to stop myself from crying out, 'My Anu, I want her, I want her back.'

I feel the quickening in my womb . . .

I'm too tired to go on any more, I feel I've reached the limits of exhaustion, I must get to bed. But this breathlessness, this heaviness in my chest – is it only exhaustion? As I get up from Kartik's bedside, I realise it's my asthma again. And this time, there's no fear. I feel amazingly clear-headed, all the confusion gone.

PART FOUR

Standing still I searched,
Stretching out my arms,
Sinking deep into the earth,
Like the banyan roots,
Seeking the spring of life.

'Urmi, they're here,' Inni calls out.

As always, Vanaa and the girls usher in chaos. Akka is the last to enter, Kartik and Mandira clustering about her, both of them speaking to her at the same time; but it is at me she looks, over and above all the others. Her look is like a question, it is as if she is asking me 'How are you?' I smile and she turns away to greet Inni. I can see that Inni is slightly tense; she is always apprehensive about Akka's visit and so is Akka. If Inni finds Akka's air of calm strength formidable, Akka is intimidated by Inni's beauty and sophistication. I used to have my own doubts earlier about bringing them together, my mother and my mother-in-law, two women wholly unlike, having nothing in common. But after the initial hiccups, they get on well together. 'Like oil and water,' Kishore had said once. 'They don't mix, but it's a peaceful combination.'

'Seven pieces of luggage for one person,' Harish exclaims, putting down the larger bags.

'Most of it is for you people,' Akka says apologetically.

151

'Don't we know that! Why do you think Pallavi's clinging to that bag? She thinks her birthday present is in that.'

'Is it? Akka, show us what you've got for Pallavi. And for Kartik.'

'I have something for you too, Mandira. But not now. After my bath.'

Harish is staying on for lunch, and he is unusually relaxed, never once looking at his watch, or showing any impatience with the chaos. It's Vanaa who's nervous, wanting to have the lunch on time, arranging the table in a formal manner, even, to my astonishment, bringing out some table mats from somewhere.

'There!' I say to Harish when we finally settle down at the table. 'This is all in your honour. I hope it comes up to your standard.'

Harish smiles a distant smile – he doesn't like jokes about these matters – and Vanaa gives me a quick warning look. He leaves us the moment lunch is over and we continue to sit round the table while Akka has her meal – she refuses to have it with her son-in-law, and won't let any of us wait with her, either – the debris of our lunch all about us. The talk inevitably turns to Ranidurg. Akka tells us about the controversy that's rocking Ranidurg over the installation of the statue of our warrior queen.

'It has to be in the central square, but it's so crowded, there's no place left, not an inch. They already have Gandhiji, Nehru, Ambedkar, and there was Indira last year . . .'

We laugh, we argue animatedly, but Inni, who knows very little of Ranidurg, feels left out. Her lugubrious face makes us uncomfortable. When the phone rings, she gets up with alacrity.

'That will be for me,' she says. But a moment later she calls out to me. 'Urmi, it's for you.'

It's Bhaskar, inviting me to his home for lunch. 'I thought

Thursday, perhaps. I have an off, and I know you're having vacations . . .'

'Vacations, yes, but we have work – exams, corrections, etc., etc. And besides . . .' I tell him about Akka's visit and the children's birthdays.

'Well, tell me what day is convenient.'

I am vague, but he is insistent, he won't let me off. I find it a bit tiresome, but finally agree to a day.

'That was Bhaskar,' I tell Vanaa who looks inquiringly at me when I return. 'He's invited me home for lunch.'

'Oh!' That's all. But I catch her exchange a quick glance with Inni and there's a small silence immediately after. Not for the first time it occurs to me that they think I'm getting involved with Bhaskar. I have a presentiment Vanaa's going to speak to me about it – I hear her whispering with Inni – but Akka is with us and she desists.

After lunch I ask Akka about Balkaka who hasn't been well.

'He's better now, but still very weak. He can't really manage himself now, Urmi. I told him I'd send him his meals – it's no problem for me to cook a little more – but he refuses. And you know why? Because of what people will say.' Vanaa giggles. 'Yes, laugh, it's funny, isn't it, two old people like us having to face such rubbish. I told him he should ignore these things, but he's stubborn.'

'Look who's talking!'

This is Vanaa's cue for starting on her 'you can't live alone, you must come and stay with us,' speech. Akka and I listen to her tirade in silence, and after a while she turns to me in irritation. 'Say something, why don't you? Sitting there like a Mummy!'

'You mean a Sphinx,' Akka murmurs.

'You know you'd like Akka to live with us.'

Do I? I think of that dream of mine, of all of us living together, even Balkaka, so that I never have to worry

153

about any of them, everyone under my eyes. No more guilt about anyone. But Akka, Balkaka and Inni under one roof? And Kishore? What about Kishore who can't stay more than a few days in a place? How do I fit him into this dream of mine?

'The way this silly girl talks, as if I'm senile and dying! I know the day will come when I can't manage myself and then I'm on your heads. But until then . . .'

'But Akka . . .'

'That's enough, you stupid girl.'

'Silly girl, stupid girl . . . For God's sake, Akka, I'm a woman. At least allow me that, even if you refuse to give me credit for any sense. You talk to me as if I'm Pallavi.'

'You sound like Pallavi right now.'

'Mothers and daughters, mothers and daughters,' I say reprovingly and suddenly stop. Vanaa continues to sulk. After a studied silence she looks at her watch, gets up, pulls out her pleats, rearranges them on her fingers, tucks them back in, adjusts her *pallu* – such obvious preparations that Akka asks, 'Where are you going?'

'I must go home,' she says.

'Harish said . . .' I began mockingly.

She glares at me, but when Akka affectionately pulls her down, saying, 'Oh, don't go, Vanu, I won't let you,' she subsides back on the bed.

Only at night, after Inni and Kartik have gone to bed, does Akka ask me the question she'd left unasked in the morning. 'And how are you, Urmi?'

'Physically I'm all right, as you see. But sometimes, like this morning, when Vanaa and you were arguing, I think I've lost it all and suddenly it comes up here.' I put my hand to my throat.

'Vanaa wrote to me she wasn't sure you'd be celebrating the children's birthdays, but I knew you'd want to go on normally.'

'Now, yes. But at first I thought, if I stop grieving, if I take up my normal life, I'll be betraying Anu.'

'You can't hold on to your grief that way, you have to let it go. Only then our dead stay with us.'

How does she know? It's true. I realised it in Hardwar, after Amrut and I had immersed Papa's ashes. We lit our flowery lamps and set them afloat in the river. Night came down upon us as we sat in silence and watched the twinkling cavalcade of lights drift serenely past us and into the darkness. Peace fell upon me then as if I had let go all the pain of Papa's death. And there was something else, a strange feeling that Papa was there with us.

Yes, Akka is right, our dead are always with us. I have tried not to be snagged on to the past, to leave it behind and go on. 'How many children do you have?' Lalita asked me. 'One,' I said. That was unforgivable. Death cannot blot out life. Anu will always be with me. The link between us stays vibrant, alive. A kind of comforting warmth suffuses me at the thought, thawing the chill that has been with me since Anu died.

Suddenly I decide. I will tell Akka about Mira, about my dream, no, it is no longer just a dream, it is a plan, to resurrect Mira, to let her voice be heard. Akka listens to me in silence.

'Can I read the poems?' she asks when I've done.

It is almost midnight when she comes to the end. For a long time she sits staring at the papers. What is it she's seeing? Finally she smooths the papers, sighs and looks at me.

'I was twenty-seven when I got married. In those days, it was old. My family thought I was a hopeless case, I'd be a burden on them forever. When this offer came, they were jubilant. But I was afraid. How could I look after another woman's child? But . . .' She pauses, I can sense her coming back to the present.

155

'You want to publish these in Kannada?' she asks.

'Of course.'

'But you've translated them into English.'

Instinctively my hand goes to cover the papers, clumsily trying to conceal them. 'Oh, these. They're for myself. I felt I could understand them better,' I confess shame-facedly, 'if I saw them in English. But they have to be published in the original. That's why I'm coming to Ranidurg as soon as our vacations begin, Kartik's and mine. Do you know anyone who might publish them?'

She thinks for a moment. 'There's Vidya's father – she was my student. I'll talk to him. You'll be coming in April, I suppose? Kishore will be here by then.'

Yes, Kishore will be here. How strange, I haven't thought of his return. For the first time since my marriage, I haven't crossed out the days to his return.

'Have you thought of what Kishore will say to this plan of yours?' Akka asks anxiously.

I try to think. 'I don't know,' I confess to Akka finally.

She's very different from what I'd imagined Bhaskar's mother would be. It's not just that she's totally unlike him – this woman is thin, emaciated almost, her blouse hanging on her as if she's lost weight recently – it's her manner. She has nothing of his air of ease. She's restless, she fusses over me, apologising effusively for her husband's absence, as if he has slighted me by not being at home. Bhaskar sits silent meanwhile, drumming his fingers on the arms of his chair, quite unembarrassed by her flow of talk. Ignoring him, she thrusts her untidy, straggling hair off her face and begins to question me. Her questions remind me of the way Bhaskar had prowled in our living room on the first day he had come home, of the way he had picked up things and examined them. She is as unselfconscious and direct as he was, but my polite smile soon drops off. There is something

156

tiring about her directness; she demands answers, she won't be fobbed off.

'Merchant Navy? What do you need a job for then?' she exclaims when I tell her about Kishore's job. 'Your husband must be earning a lot of money. Give up your job, give it up,' she says airily, waving her hands. I notice how unexpectedly large her wrists and hands are and how clumsy and ungainly they look at the end of her thin arms.

'My Ma's the despair of any feminist. I'd like your friend with the three names to make something of her.'

'Who? Priti?' she asks him.

I'd told him about Priti hyphenating her maiden and marriage names. He must have passed it on to her, he tells her everything. For some reason the thought is disquieting.

A girl comes in with some drinks. It gives me a respite. I look round the room, noticing that there's nothing about to show his mother's love of music, unless Bhaskar's habit of drumming is a vestigial ghost of it. And I remember his telling me, 'She changed completely after my sister died.' So have I, perhaps. But my daughter and hers – they stay where they were, what they were. Yet Anu hated stillness. She was restless, she could never stay in one place. For a few days we tried confining her within a playpen. She was wretched, tugging at us when we went near her, demanding to be taken out. And when she was released, how loudly she proclaimed her joy in chortling laughter, in her quick-silver movements as she crawled all over the house!

It's all over now, my love for her, my joy in her, my dreams about her. And this woman? How has she coped? What's there for her now?

As if Bhaskar has caught at my thought, he begins to tell me, in a teasing tone, of his mother's addiction to old movies. 'She sees one a day, sometimes even two. She's crazy about Raj Kapoor and Nargis . . .'

'Go on, make fun of me, but tell me, have you anything

157

like them now? What a pair they were, huh? And Madhu-bala, is there anyone now to touch her for beauty?'

'Okay, Ma, we grant it to you, we have nothing to equal those marvels of yours.'

I sit back and listen to their gentle sparring, relaxed, without the force of her attention on me. But when we start lunch, she turns to me once again. It's not very comfortable. She's one of those over-hospitable hosts, convinced that guests, unless they're forced to eat, will go home starving. I find this insistence irritating. Perhaps Bhaskar realises it, for he suddenly takes charge of the situation.

'Leave her alone, Ma, and look after yourself. You eat like a sparrow yourself and expect others to gorge themselves.'

She subsides into silence and as if he has got his cue, Bhaskar takes over. His look, as always, draws things out of me, but his mother's presence is somehow inhibiting. It's not that she is hostile, far from it, nor is she disinterested. It's the very steadiness of her gaze on my face, the ingenuous look as she listens to me, that makes it hard for me to talk easily. She is silent, but I know she's opted out of the conversation voluntarily; if she wants to join in, she will. And she does, swiftly retorting to a light remark I make about Bhaskar, as if I have accused him of something. 'My Bhaskar can do anything he has a mind to do.'

'Oh Ma, you can't bear a word against your son, can you?'

There is such a filmy flavour to this, I immediately think, I must tell Amrut this. But no, we can't laugh at them, this relationship is real.

'Am I wrong, Urmila?' she appeals to me. 'You have a son, you know what mothers feel like.'

She seems to be making an effort to bind us together,

158

both of us mothers, and the sense of having offended her vanishes.

Nevertheless, I am not comfortable. And it is only when I am leaving that I suddenly realise what it is that has made me uneasy.

'Come on, I'll drop you home,' Bhaskar says.

'You don't have to. I can see you're dying for your nap.'

'I am and I wouldn't give it up for many people, but I'll sacrifice it for you.'

'He's a flatterer, my Bhaskar. Don't take him seriously, be careful, Urmila, be careful,' his mother says, wagging a playful finger at me.

There's something about her – what is it? Whatever it is, I don't like it. They realise I'm displeased. 'Go then,' she says to him sternly. 'What are you standing here for? Go and drop her home.'

I no longer protest. To do so is to make an issue of something that isn't very important. Not to me, anyway. I say my thanks to her, but I have a feeling she isn't listening. When I have done, she picks up my plait that's flopped over my shoulder and says, 'Lovely hair.'

Just that! 'Lovely hair', in a tone of grudging admiration. And in a flash it comes to me – she's been inspecting me, like a mother with a girl her son wants to marry. It's so bizarre a thought I have to remind myself – I'm a married woman with a six-year-old son, she knows that, for God's sake. But the impression remains.

When we get into the car, Bhaskar, as if apologising, no, not apologising, explaining her, says, 'I have to live for Jyoti as well. Can you understand that? My mother has never let her go. I have to live for two people. Can you understand that?'

'Yes,' I say, 'I understand.' But I can't. How can she burden him with this? It frightens me.

159

I wait for him to start the car, but he sits staring before him.

'My mother wants me to get married,' he says suddenly.

'Naturally. Like all good mothers.'

He does not smile. 'She's been preparing for it for years, ever since I passed my finals. She's very business-like about it. She's got a list of eligible girls from our community. Whenever a girl gets married, she strikes off her name. And she's always including new names in her list. She has their photographs as well.'

'Really, Bhaskar!' I am appalled. 'I can't believe anyone does things this way.'

'Why not?' He gives me a defiant look. All his good humour seems to have disappeared. 'Tell me, what's wrong with it? You believe in marriage-for-love, you think only that is right?'

'It's not that, it's just . . . this seems so cold-blooded. As if those girls are objects in a catalogue. You know what I mean.'

'It's sensible.' I'm silent. 'And it gives my mother such pleasure, all those possibilities. Tell me, what's wrong with that?'

'It leaves out the girls. Girls aren't going to meekly accept any man their parents choose for them – not any more. What if the girl your mother chooses for you refuses you? Has she thought of that?'

'My mother think of any girl refusing me! Ha!' He is smiling now, but there's a kind of self-mockery in it. 'I'm the only son of rich parents, a highly qualified man – how can any girl refuse me? No, no, it can't happen, it's impossible. My mother wants a "Sweet, homely, fair, convent-educated girl" for me, and she'll get her, never fear.'

'So there are no problems.'

'None. Except that I've gone and fallen in love with a dark, sharp-tongued, married woman.'

The switch from the light-hearted to this is done so easily, with no change in his tone at all, that I'm taken wholly unawares.

'Well,' I say at last, feebly, with a laugh, but the laugh comes off more awkwardly than I'd intended, 'What will your mother say?'

'You never speak of your husband.' It's like an accusation.

'Should I?'

'Most women do.'

He waits for my reply. When there's none, he leans forward and takes off my glasses.

'What's that for?'

'I want to see your eyes. I want to see you without your shield.'

He says this with such feeling, he looks at me with such intensity, it brings out the goose bumps on my arms. For the first time, I'm frightened. I have to force myself to speak.

'Caveman stuff.' I pick up my glasses, put them on. 'Must be the influence of all those movies your mother watches.'

'Tell me about your marriage.'

He sees the 'why?' in my eyes perhaps, for he says, as if explaining, 'It's the most important thing to me right now.'

I can say nothing. The silence stretches between us, becomes painful. His face is bleak. Has he realised he does not figure anywhere in the equation of my marriage?

'You love him.'

I can feel myself flush, I can feel the heat move over my face as the blood courses through it. His eyes, fastened on my face, seem to be following the trail of that flush. He waits for a while, then starts the car and drives me home in silence.

I'm feeling cheated. Bhaskar has no business stepping outside the role I've allotted to him in my life. I don't really know what his role is to be, but certainly it's not this, not that of a lover. No, it's not Bhaskar, it's really myself I'm angry with. I have no excuse for not knowing. I tried to close my eyes, but Vanaa and Inni have been warning me.

'Oh, Inni likes to exaggerate,' I said when Vanaa told me.

'Inni's worried about you; about you and – I mean your friendship with Bhaskar,' Vanaa had said awkwardly.

'Oh, Inni! If I have to live by her rules . . .'

'But Urmi . . .'

I wouldn't let her talk, I laughed at her and Inni, I pooh-poohed their fears. 'And don't pry into my sexual life,' I said sternly. 'Do I pry into yours?'

She blushed at that, but she didn't, as I had expected her to, give up and change the subject. She persisted.

'Urmi, you should realise he's serious about you. Have you heard him say your name?'

'Don't worry, Vanaa,' I reassured her, seeing she was truly concerned. 'I'm quite safe. I have my blade of grass.'

'Blade of grass?' She was puzzled.

'Like Sita,' I added.

'Oh!' she said then, as if she understood. But I wonder if she really did. I know what she thinks I meant. I love Kishore and therefore . . .

Is that my blade of grass? Bhaskar obviously thinks so too. 'You love him?' he asked, and how anxiously he looked into my face as if the relationship between us hinged on my reply to his question. Why didn't I tell him the truth?

I fell in love with Kishore when I was fifteen. 'Fell in love', what a flabby, over-used phrase it is. But that's exactly how

162

it was for me – I fell headlong into that emotion in a moment. There was the same sensation of being shaken, of breathlessness that there is after a fall. Until then, he had been only Kishore, Vanaa's rather strange, aloof brother. And then suddenly, as if someone had drawn a circle about him, he was singled out from the rest of humanity for me. I can remember not only the day, but the exact moment this happened. It was the day my grandfather died.

I was sitting on the steps outside our house when Kishore came on his motor-cycle. He said something I couldn't hear because of the roar of his engine. He saw my blank look and shut it off. In the silence I could hear it again, the monotonous heavy dull sound. Or was it only in my head?

'What's the matter? Locked out?'

I shook my head.

'Akka sent me to tell you . . .' Then he saw my face. 'What is the matter?'

I told him then about the noise, a kind of irregular, rhythmic heavy sound from the passage.

'And the doors of the passage – both of them – are bolted from inside. I've knocked and banged, but . . . And I can't find Aju anywhere . . .'

'Wait here,' he said and ran in. I heard the clatter of his shoes on the floor. I tried to get up, to follow him in, but I had been sitting for so long that my legs crumpled under me. I would have fallen, if Kishore, coming back, hadn't supported me.

'You can't . . .?'

'No, I'll have to get some others. Come home with me.'

I refused and he didn't argue. I sat in the kitchen while they broke open the passage door. Kishore's face, when he came to me, told me the truth.

'He's dead.'

'Yes.'

'How?'

He hesitated, but only a moment. 'He's hanged himself.'

I refused to leave the house – how could I, until Papa came? – so Akka came to me. It was sheer exhaustion finally that made me go to bed. Akka sat by me, she was still there when I fell asleep. When I woke up, she had gone, and Kishore was there instead. He was reading, totally absorbed in his book, his face calm and beautiful. It was at that precise moment that I fell in love with him. And when, on my eighteenth birthday, I got his letter, I had a sense of having willed his feelings into being by the strength of my own. I can remember how I waited for him that day at my hostel gate, from early afternoon on. And how, when I saw him hours later, getting out of a taxi, I ran across the road, uncaring of the traffic and threw myself into his arms.

'You love him?' Bhaskar asked me and I flushed. He thought he had his answer. I love my husband and therefore I am an inviolate, chaste Sita. Vanaa thinks so too. 'Oh!' she said, as if she understood.

But how can Vanaa, secure in the fortress of her marriage to Harish, understand what it is like – marriage with a man who flits into my life a few months in a year and flits out again, leaving nothing of himself behind? Often, after he has gone, I find in myself a frantic grappling for his image, as if in going he has taken that away as well. Then he returns and we pick up the course of our lives from the moment of his return. Both of us behave – at least, he's always done, and I've learnt to do so – as if there is only this present. Neither the past nor the future have any place in our life together; we reject both. And in this world of 'now' that we inhabit, passion between us remains intact.

Then he goes away and I'm left with that passion. There was a time when I was frightened by the intensity of my bodily hungers for Kishore. It seemed to do nothing but complicate my life enormously. I often wished I could put my desires into a deep freeze and take them out, intact and whole, when he returned. I remember a day when Harish and Vanaa were driving me home. I saw Vanaa rest her cheek lightly on Harish's arm, a slight gesture to which Harish instantly responded. They looked at each other and I thought, they will make love when they go home. Pain slashed through me and I knew then how vulnerable I was. I tried after that to control the erotic fantasies that invaded me in the early hours of the morning, fantasies in which I wove, in great detail, different patterns of love-making; but I soon realised the only way I could come to terms with my sexuality was to recognise it. Now it's no longer necessary. Since Anu's death, my body has been quiescent. Even Kishore . . . I knew it the day before he left. He held me close that night and I felt his body respond to that closeness, but my own recoiled; it was an instinctive recoil. He felt it and let me go. He did not touch me after that. Yes, I was honest when I told Vanaa 'I'm safe'.

And yet for a moment I was tempted, I was perilously close to responding to Bhaskar, to giving him what he wants. It was like the time in the hostel when they had dared me to get out on to the ledge outside my window to pick up a book I'd dropped. I'd jumped out, and to shock them even more, had walked along the narrow ledge and round the corner. And there, high above the ground, with nothing, it seemed, between me and the stretch of open sea, with the wind buffeting at my body, making me sway, I forgot everything. There was only the heady feeling of being in total control of myself – I could not, I would never fall – of feeling really free.

But I can no longer try such stunts. I am now twelve years older. And this time I will not see the sea, but the anxious faces at the window behind me.

And yet it seems to me that this, responding to Bhaskar, is the only way of releasing the mushy adolescent with her dreams of 'living happily ever after with Kishore', who's

165

trapped inside me, of finding out what's left when she's gone.

And what about Bhaskar then? Oh, I don't know. It's so much easier, so much simpler, to just think of virtue and chastity and being a good wife. I see the point of it now.

She is alone, on her usual bench, but her tensely poised posture, like an athlete on the starting block, tells me something is wrong. The look of relief that floods her face when she sees me, the way she springs up from her seat, confirm my surmise.

'Urmila, help me, they're sending Kalpana away.'

She is frantic, incoherent and it is some time before I can make enough sense of her garbled words to understand what she is saying.

'Sending her home? You mean, they're discharging her?'

'No, they're sending her to another hospital, they tell me they can't keep her here any longer. What am I to do, Urmila? I can't go there, it's too far, even to come here is hard. How much money it's going to cost me to go there every day, and how will I be able to find the time? When I said this, they told me, take her home then. How can I, Urmila? She'll die, she'll just die.'

It is hard, almost impossible to console her. 'Have you spoken to Vanaa?' I ask her.

'No, I was waiting for you, I thought I'll say something wrong, maybe I'll make things worse . . .'

'You wait here, I'll see if Vanaa is there, I'll find out what the problem is.'

Vanaa's getting ready to leave. She's surprised to see me, smiles, then seeing my face says, 'It's about Kalpana, I suppose.'

'You know about it. You know they're throwing her out.'

She's embarrassed, I can see that.

'They're not throwing her out, they're just transferring

166

her to a suburban hospital. Look, I spoke to the AO – they
need the bed, there are just fifteen in that ward, she's been
here four months already. And there's nothing more they
can do for Kalpana here. She needs nursing, that's all.
That's just as good in the other place.'

'And what about the mother? How can she go there
every day?'

'You can't expect them to think of that. Be reasonable,
Urmi.'

'She says when she protested they said she could take
the girl home.'

'Oh, that was . . . you know how it is sometimes when
you're harassed.'

'And what about Shakutai's state? Have you seen her?
She'll die, she keeps saying.'

'And would that be such a terrible thing?'

'You don't know what you're saying, Vanaa. Not a
terrible thing for the girl to die? You think the mother can
see it that way? You know nothing about it, you shouldn't
talk.'

She flinches as if I've struck her, then controls herself
with an effort. 'I'm just doing a job here, you know I can't
do a thing. I spoke to the AO, but once these people take a
decision . . . It's no use your quarrelling with me, Urmi. If
I could do anything to help, I would.'

'I know, but it seems so unfair. Pushing a girl like that
around. Not enough beds!'

'Would you like to see the AO yourself? I warn you,
though, it's no use. I have enough experience of
administrators.'

Shakutai's face falls when she sees me. I don't need to
tell her I've not been able to do anything.

'What about that Jain doctor, Urmila?' she asks me.

'I don't think he can help. These things are not in the
doctor's hands. And anyway, he's a very junior doctor.'

167

'What shall I do, Urmila, what shall I do?' Her hands clutch mine, I can feel the tremor in them. 'You go home, Urmila,' she says in a while, 'it's no use your waiting here.'

But I am reluctant to leave her alone, I am standing helplessly by her when I hear someone call my name.

'Malcolm! What are you doing here?'

'I could ask you the same question.' He looks curiously at Shakutai. 'I came here to see someone, he was supposed to give me a story. But the chap's got himself discharged. It was gang warfare,' he tells me with such sang-froid that I have to laugh.

'Is that funny? You wouldn't think so if you'd seen what they did to this guy. Just drew a knife from here to here . . .' He whistles as he shows me the way it was done.

'I thought you were on the way to being a crusading journalist?'

'Instead of which I am chasing two-paisa hoodlums for their stories, eh? That's life. Anyway, I have to go and trace this fellow. I can't go back without a story. The trouble is, these chaps are scared of the press . . .'

Something clicks in my mind when he says that. 'Malcolm, can you do me a favour? Will you wait here just a minute? Don't go, I'll be back.'

I go back to Shakutai who has been watching us curiously.

'Shakutai, listen to me, this man is my friend, we were in college together, he's working for a newspaper now. Are you prepared to tell him about Kalpana?'

'Tell him about Kalpana,' she repeats, bewildered.

'He'll print it in the papers, what they're doing to her, the way they're putting her out because there are no beds!'

'In the papers? Then everyone will know.'

'Yes. But this is the only way. You know what happens once things get into the papers. They won't be able to touch Kalpana.'

168

Shakutai hesitates. I wait patiently for her to make up her mind but Malcolm, getting impatient perhaps, comes to us. 'What is it, Urmila?'

I make a gesture asking him to wait. Shakutai looks up at him, then at me – an earnest and searching kind of look. 'It will help Kalpana?'

'It might.'

At last she says, 'All right.'

'Malcolm, this is Shakutai, her daughter is a patient here . . . Tell him about it yourself, Shakutai.'

'What is wrong with your daughter?' Malcolm asks in polite disinterest. He'll listen only because I've asked him to.

Shakutai falters, looks at me, finally says, 'It was an accident.'

Sensing something, Malcolm waits for her to go on. 'Car accident?' he prompts her when she doesn't.

'You tell him, Urmila,' Shakutai pleads with me.

'What shall I tell him?'

She is silent for a moment. 'Whatever you think you should – to help Kalpana.' The words seem to be forced out of her.

I hesitate, then turn away from her. 'She was raped,' I tell Malcolm. I have spoken in English, but Shakutai's face tells me she knows what I've said.

'Raped!' Suddenly alert, he listens to me attentively.

'Do you think I've done the right thing?' Shakutai asks me when he's gone. Before I can think of what to say to her, she stands up, hurriedly pushing her feet into her *chappals*. 'Doctorsaheb is coming,' she says.

It's Bhaskar. I haven't seen him since the day we parted in the car. He responds to Shakutai's greeting before he turns to me and says 'hello'. Just that, not even a smile. Nor does he say my name. There's something cold and unbending about him. I wait a moment for him to say any

169

more, but he doesn't. He just swings around and walks away. It hurts. And anger throbs in me. What the hell, why does he have to do it this way? Why can't he be reasonable? Reasonable? What do I mean? I have to laugh at myself.

Well, that's over, I tell myself when I'm in the bus. He's like all men. If he can't get what he wants . . . But suddenly, thinking of how he looked as he walked away – even his back looked desolate – tears well into my eyes, taking me unawares. I fumble for a kerchief, but I can't find one. And I'm not even wearing a sari I can weep into. I give up and let the tears splosh coldly down my cheeks and on to my hands.

I am sitting with the Sunday papers spread about me when Vanaa calls. 'Have you seen the papers?'

'I'm just reading . . .'

'The bit about Kalpana?'

'Yes, I've seen it. I knew about it, actually . . .'

'You knew? What do you mean?'

'It was Malcolm – you remember he was in my class . . .'

'You told him about it, you did that?' She doesn't let me reply but goes on swiftly herself. 'Urmi, I'm coming there, I'll be right over, wait for me.'

I am puzzled. No, more than puzzled, I am disturbed. Vanaa sounded menacing. Vanaa threatening me? I have a sinking feeling.

I don't have to wait long. She goes straight to the point. 'Why did you do it?'

'Do what? Tell Malcolm, you mean? What else could we do?'

'What good have you done her? Look at this . . .' She stabs angrily at the picture – she's brought a copy of the paper with her – holding it before me as if it's evidence that's going to incriminate me. I recognise the picture. 'She was dressed up, lipstick and all.' It's the one with her

170

friend, though the other girl has been cut out. 'It's all over for the girl and her family now. You know how frightened she was of people coming to know.'

'I asked her before we spoke to Malcolm, it was her decision.'

'Hers! What does she understand? You know what she thinks of you, she thinks you're . . . oh, God Himself. You've taken advantage of that. It's not fair.'

'Not fair! And was it fair for the girl to be thrown out of the hospital because there are not enough beds! Was it fair for her to be raped that way? Imagine what that girl has gone through . . .'

'That's not the point, let's not speak of that now.'

'No, of course not, it's so ugly, let's all look the other way, it's none of our business, anyway.'

'Does it help the girl to be exposed like this?'

'What do you mean exposed?' I turn on her in fury. 'You talk as if she's the one who's done wrong.'

'Wrong, right . . . You talk like a child, Urmi.'

'Listen to me, Vanaa . . .'

But Vanaa is not prepared to listen. I realise with a pang of something approaching fear that I've never seen her this way before. For the first time, since the day she took my hand and led me home, I feel our relationship threatened. She goes on and on, it's incredible, she dredges up things from the past I've forgotten myself, she brings in Josephine from our schooldays, she accuses me of being influenced by Priti, of wanting to become a do-gooder who needs victims . . .

There is a sense of being battered, bludgeoned. I don't speak, I don't want to any more, I can't. I only listen, some part of my mind registering the words, though after a while they mean nothing. There is a feeling of utter desolation. That dream of mine, all of us living together, lies shattered

171

about me, the smooth silvery surface splintered into a million cruelly sharp pieces.

And then she speaks of Akka. 'You're so insensitive, how could you ask Akka to help you with the poems? Didn't you imagine what she would feel? You saw her that day when she read them, you saw how she cried. And to talk of publishing them – how can you, Urmi, how can you! It's all right for you and me, we don't live there. But Akka does. Once people read those poems, how can she hold her head up again? You heard her, you heard what she said about Balkaka.'

Vanaa was with me when Baiajji died, she held my hand when Kartik was being born, she stayed with me through all those dark days after Anu's death. And now she is letting go. No, I won't let her, I won't let that happen.

'Vanaa, stop it, stop it at once,' I raise my voice above hers. She stops speaking with a shocking abruptness, looks at me and bursts into tears. I wait, silent, until the storm of weeping is over. Her eyes are red, her face moist and flaccid with much weeping.

'I'm sorry,' she mumbles with the directness of a penitent child.

'I'm sorry, but sometimes,' she suddenly speaks with more spirit, 'you need someone to say these things to you. You're so impetuous. Remember the time in the hostel you ran down to help the man we thought had fainted, and what he did to you?'

'Vanaa,' I kneel down by her and gently ask her, 'it's the poems, isn't it? It's the poems you're angry about.'

'It's Kalpana, too,' she says stubbornly.

'Yes, but mainly it's Mira. Why should it hurt you so, Vanaa? You know there isn't a single reason why Akka shouldn't be able to hold up her head.'

'He was my father,' she says. Her eyes fill with tears again.

'I know that. I know he was Kishore's father, too.'

172

'It all happened so long ago. Why do you need to rake it up? Why? What do you want?'

What do I want? I repeat the question and Mira's words come back to me:

What do I want, I ask myself.
The mind-slate wiped clean
mocks me with its blankness.

No, I have to give Vanaa an answer, I owe her that.

I get up abruptly and begin to walk about. I can feel her eyes following my movements.

'You know, Vanaa, after Baiajji died and Aju wanted us to go on as before, he asked me, "We can manage, can't we?" And I said, so confidently, "Yes, we can manage". But it was not easy, you know that, Vanaa. No, you don't, you were away then. Aju became strange, sometimes for days he wouldn't say a word. Without Baiajji he became a shadow. There were so many things I couldn't cope with. You remember that cook of ours? I knew she was stealing, and her son used to leave dirty pictures in my books. And there was the 'other family' – they kept coming but Aju refused to meet them, so I had to. They made such sly insinuations, I hated it, but I said nothing, for if I did it would mean I couldn't cope. And when I decided to marry Kishore,' I go back to her and as I speak I play with the bangles on her wrist, the musical tinkle becoming a kind of accompaniment to my words, 'Papa asked me, "Are you sure you can manage, Urmi? He won't be home most of the time." You asked me too, "Are you sure? You know how Kishore is," you said. And I said it to all of you, "Yes, I can manage." I have, haven't I? I've earned money, looked after the children and Papa when he was ill and Inni . . . And all the time, it's like there's been a voice inside me saying, "Urmi's so smart, so competent".'

173

Vanaa looks at me questioningly, and I force myself to go on.

'After Anu died, the voice stopped. Then I saw Kalpana, I met Shakutai, I read Mira's diary, her poems. And I've begun to think yes, I've managed, but I've been lucky, that's all. While these women . . . You understand what I'm saying, Vanaa? They never had a chance. It's not fair, it's not fair at all. And we can't go on pushing it – what happened to them – under the carpet forever because we're afraid of disgrace.' I look directly into her face now. 'Have I answered your question?'

Vanaa's face is blank. She is silent. I wait patiently for her reply. Finally she gives herself a small shake, sighs. And I relax. The danger is past.

'For years I kept hoping that my father would begin to know me, to love me. And then I saw you and your father together. You cleared up the house after your grandfather died, do you remember? You were there for a month, just the two of you. After seeing you, I knew my father didn't love me, no, he would never love me. I gave up that hope then.'

Tears well up in her eyes once again.

'Oh, stop it.' I shake her. 'And listen, Vanaa, I want you to read Mira's poems.'

'I will. Sometime.'

'No, today. Now.'

She smiles, a faint, watery smile, at my enthusiasm and asks the same question Akka had, 'And what will Kishore say?'

I've worked hard at knowing Mira, I've read her diaries, gone through her papers, absorbed her poems, painfully, laboriously translated them into English. And now, I tell myself, I know Mira.

But Kishore? What will Kishore say? I try to think and there's only blankness – the same blankness that confronted

174

me when Bhaskar said 'Tell me about your marriage'. Have I never let Kishore become part of my real world? 'There's nothing of you here,' Bhaskar had said to me; looking about me, contrasting the bareness of this room to the muddle of my room in Ranidurg, I realise he's right. Even the bedcovers, faded to a bleached softness with much washing, have been bought for me by Vanaa.

What will Kishore say? I must know the answer. It matters to me, to us.

'I don't know what Kishore will say,' I tell Vanaa. 'But I'll write to him, I'll tell him what I'm going to do, what I think and feel. And I'll wait to see what he says. I can't do more than that, can I?'

She looks doubtfully at me. 'And what if he says, "No, you can't do this"?'

I have to think this over. It takes me a long time to say, 'I'll cross that bridge when I come to it.'

Shakutai is not alone. I guess, from the aura of effortless intimacy that surrounds them, that he is her husband. And I am right. Smiling affectionately at me she says, 'This is Kalpana's father.'

For some reason I had imagined him to be a crushed, feeble kind of a man. This man, however, has a pleasingly dapper look. He seems, too, in some way untouched by life; which is why, perhaps, he appears younger than his wife.

'This is, you know, Urmilatai, I told you about her,' Shakutai tells him.

He gets up and greets me with a *namaste*. I do the same. An awkward silence falls over us. It is he who speaks first. 'You've come to see my girl?' he asks. While I hesitate, he goes on, 'Look at her. He should have killed her, the bastard. I wish I could get my hands on him.'

'That's enough of your heroics,' his wife says dryly. 'You think this is a film?'

He gives her a look and I see with shock that he has tears in his eyes. He wipes them and mumbles, 'I must go', but makes no move to do so. We continue to stand in silence.

'Go then, if you're going,' his wife impatiently says.

He puts his hand in his pocket and fishes out a small plastic bag. 'Take this, it's some *khau* for Sandhya.' He calls it '*khau*' using the child's word for sweets.

'*Khau!*' she repeats bitterly. 'She's not a baby.'

'Give it to her, she'll eat it.'

'All right.'

'I'll come tomorrow.'

'All right.'

He makes an awkward gesture of farewell towards me and mumbling something walks away.

'We went to see an astrologer,' Shakutai tells me. 'He said we should go and ask about Kalpana, he said this man is very good, somebody told him that. There was such a crowd there, Urmila, it was like an ST bus stand. We had to wait for three hours before we could see him. Imagine! And you know what he said? He said Kalpana's stars are very bad, the evil influences are very strong; but he says the bad period is coming to an end. Soon she will recover, become normal. I don't know,' she seems suddenly uncertain, then cheers up again. 'All the people who were talking to us when we were waiting said the man is very good, his predictions always come right. What do you think, Urmila?' she asks me anxiously, as if it matters to her what I say, 'Do you think people can really know what's going to happen?'

'Next year all will be well,' she used to say in a booming voice – the astrologer in whose house I stayed a few months before my marriage. 'Next year all will be well:

176

your daughter will be married, your son will turn over a new leaf, pass his exams, your husband/wife will recover . . .' What if I had gone to her last year, when Anu was a baby in the cradle, her lips dewy with milk? Would she have said the same to me, 'Next year, all will be well?'

'No,' my voice comes out harsh, 'we can never know the future. I think we shouldn't try to know it, it's not ours. Shakutai,' I come to the point she's been trying to avoid, 'is it very bad?'

She gives me a look and just as quickly looks away. 'I knew how it would be, I shouldn't complain. I had thought, even if my sari is torn, I can wear it so that the rents don't show, but . . . What's the use? That was not to be. Everywhere we go they look at us as if we're actors in a drama. We stay inside the house, we don't come out unless we have to. If only they hadn't put the photo, I think many people would never have known. Why did they have to put the photo, Urmila?'

'Newspapers must have photographs, you know that.'

Yes, we like to see them, the faces of the victims as well as their murderers, the mutilated bodies of accident cases, the tears of a defeated champion, the sobbing faces of anguished relatives; we're the cheering spectators watching the gladiators fight to death.

'Prakash has become difficult to deal with, even Sandhya . . . Only Sulu, only my Sulu is just the same.'

I can see her throat working. She controls herself with an effort.

'Sometimes I think, Urmila, I've had enough. What have I had all my life but troubles? I should die, I've had enough. The kind of things they are saying, the police people, about Kalpana. Such dirt. Her father cried like a child when he read it. She was a good girl, I swear to you, my Kalpana was a good girl.'

'As long as you know that, Shakutai, don't worry about what others say.'

'How can I not worry? I have to live with people, I have to live among them. I think I made a mistake, I should have kept quiet. I thought I was helping Kalpana. But sometimes I think the only thing that can help Kalpana now is death. You know, each time I come here, I keep thinking, maybe this time, when I come into this ward, I'll see an empty bed, or maybe there will be another patient in her bed and they'll tell me, "Your daughter is dead, she died last night". And for a moment, sinner that I am, my heart feels light at the thought. Then it's as if someone has hit me here and I think, what kind of a woman am I to long for my daughter's death? I, who gave her birth . . . I'll never live like you, she used to say to me, always, all the time. God has fulfilled that desire of hers. Look at her, just look at her. I gave her nothing in her life, my Kalpana, and now I've given away her name as well.'

I can say nothing to her that will take away the sting of self-reproach, because it pierces me too. Did I do wrong?

'Do you know what my greatest fear really is, Urmila? It's that she'll go on and on this way. What will we do then? What will I do? I asked the doctor about it and he said he can't give me an answer, he said even God can't. Urmila,' she suddenly seems to remember something, 'they say the doctor is in trouble. Jain doctor.'

'What has he done?'

'He told the paperwalas what really happened, that they told him not to give his report. He told them the state Kalpana was in when they brought her here. One of the sisters was telling me they might dismiss him. Can they?'

'I don't know, I don't think so.'

She sighs. We sit in silence for a while. The exodus of visitors has begun. Visiting hours are coming to an end. 'I

178

don't feel like going home now, the way people look and talk. But . . . I'll have a look at Kalpana and come.'

I follow her into the ward and realise what she meant when she spoke of being stared at. Glances follow her as if a spotlight has been focused on her. Even the nurses are looking towards her. One of them walks swiftly towards her and says something to Shakutai, her face animated. Shakutai listens, then comes to me, bewildered.

'Urmila, there's a *morcha* going on outside, sister told me about it, a lot of women are there, they're here because of Kalpana . . . where are you going Urmila?' she calls out as I move away suddenly.

'It's the best thing that could have happened,' Malcolm exclaims when he comes upon me in the mêlée. 'There's going to be so much publicity now . . .' He sees my arm. 'Urmi, you're hurt! Is it bad?'

'No,' I reassure him, 'it's nothing, only a scratch, I caught it in the crowd, that's all.' He goes away, satisfied, reluctant to spend more time on me.

The next morning I realise Malcolm was right about the publicity. The pictures of women being jostled and roughed up during the demonstration are in all the papers. The worst had happened when Kalpana was raped, I had told myself. But to Shakutai the exposure had been just as bad. Now, to see Kalpana become an issue, to see it become a game in which charges and counter-charges are exchanged is, I realise, much worse. 'Police claim Kalpana was a prostitute' one headline screams. '*Ek Kalpanechi katha?*' a headline in Marathi says, punning on Kalpana's name. Another paper brings out the fact that there are fewer beds for women in the hospital and makes that an issue. But for most of the papers, Kalpana is a victim, her family, martyrs.

'The whole world is my friend,' Shakutai says dryly. 'Can you believe it, even that woman came to see me!' She

179

sounds exactly like Baiajji saying 'those people' of Aju's first wife and her children. 'She shed a few false tears, "Poor Kalpu," she said. And, "Call me any time you need someone to sit with her." Where was she all these days! Kalpu! Kalpana never let anyone call her that. Only Sulu. And this woman . . . even he was ashamed of her. After all, he is Kalpana's father. But she . . .'

Suddenly Kalpana and her family are celebrities. The disgrace Shakutai had so agonised over wilts in the fierce glare of publicity. The final accolade on the family is bestowed when they appear, very briefly, on TV. Shakutai, sweating, nervous, stammers a few words, Sandhya and Prakash standing by her, until they are pushed out of the frame by others who shove, push, stretch their necks, even jump to get into the range of the camera.

Somehow it seems to me that the disgrace Shakutai had feared has attached itself to me. At home, I have a sense of isolation. Inni, after her first concern for my injured arm, has lapsed into a careful avoidance of the entire topic of Kalpana, which makes for a kind of strain in our relationship. Vanaa too, after one visit, stays away. I can see that her absence distresses Inni. It's hard to remember now that Inni had once objected to my association with Vanaa and her family. Now, especially after Papa's death, she's become in some way dependent on Vanaa. I hear her speaking to her on the phone and a little later, she prompts me, 'Why don't you ring her up?'

When I refuse, I know she thinks it's my pride, but it isn't. I realise Vanaa needs to take her own time.

'Don't worry, Inni, she'll come,' I reassure her.

But it's Harish who comes home that evening with Mandira. He makes it seem a casual visit, but I know it isn't. The evening, with the soothing murmur of the children's voices providing the background to our desultory but friendly conversation, is like balm to my soul. Once

Kartik and Mandira laugh loudly and the sound gladdens me. I try to say something of what I feel to Harish when he is leaving. As if I have given him an opening he refers to Vanaa for the first time. 'She's very puzzled,' he says. 'She says she never expected you to get involved in such things. Urmi's so practical, so matter-of-fact, she keeps saying.'

'But that's exactly why, I mean, it seems incredible to me that one can be so illogical, so irrational as to think that it's Kalpana who's disgraced by what's happened.'

'I wish everyone could see it that way. Anyway, don't worry, Vanaa will be all right, I know she'll turn up soon enough.'

She does. She comes with the girls the day Amrut unexpectedly arrives. The house seems noisy and cheerful once more, but it is not the same. Amrut senses the uneasiness in the atmosphere. With unusual restraint he says nothing until Vanaa has gone. Only then he asks me, 'What's wrong?'

'I can't believe it, Didi!' he exclaims when I tell him about it. 'Vanaa and you, why, you're like . . . like . . . I don't know what, but it's absolutely incredible.' He sees my face and pats my hand comfortingly. 'It's all right, she'll come round.'

'I don't know, Ambu, she's changed, she's changed a lot.'

It's as if the knowledge of what her father did, of what he was, has threatened something, disturbed the inner rhythm of her being, so that there's a sense of disharmony about her.

'Anyway,' Amrut says with an air of offering me great solace that makes me realise how very young he is, 'Radha is solidly behind you. She's sent you all kinds of messages, by the way. She even wrote a letter to the editor of "People" – did you see the awful article by that man? He calls himself a sociologist . . .'

181

'Saying that there can be no rape, because it can't be done unless the woman is willing? Yes, I've read that. And the piece by the poet who wants us to "forgive the rapist for he knows not what he is doing"! And I've read the letters that say rape happens because women go about exposing themselves. And . . . oh God! You know Amrut, sometimes I think men's minds are like public lavatories – full of dirty pictures.'

'Good Lord, Didi, what an obnoxious thought. I assure you my mind is as clean as a . . . a . . . *puja* room. I'm a good Indian boy, brought up on Hindi movies and to me all women are like my mother. Or, is it sister?' Suddenly he gets serious and asks me anxiously, 'I hope you're not going to become a man-hater, Didi?'

'That would make me one of them, wouldn't it?'

'I know. But I wish, I do wish,' he says gloomily, 'you hadn't got into this.'

'That's what Inni said once. Why did you have to get into this? It's none of your business. What is my business, Amrut? You know, Ambu, when I was expecting Anu, I told Vanaa – and I remember this every day now, every single day – once I get this over, I said, I can get on with my life. Now she's gone and it's truly over and I can get on . . . but with what?'

He looks at me in silence for a while, then says, 'Well, for a start you can get on with your PhD.'

I have to laugh. 'You're good for me, Amrut.'

'Widsom dawns at last! And I know what you mean, when people say "Mind your own business", it always makes me think of snails – crawling away blindly, you know, enclosed inside their shells. But snails get trampled over too, don't they? Squash, and it's all over for them. Nevertheless . . .'

'Yes, nevertheless . . .'

We smile at each other.

182

That night I get a call from Malcolm. 'Urmila, have you heard what happened in the Assembly today? There were questions about Kalpana, noisy scenes, I believe the women were especially loud. Anyway, what will interest you is that the Government's backtracked. They've ordered an investigation into Kalpana's case and she won't be transferred. That's great, isn't it?'

Priti's invitation was an olive branch I could not refuse; but I quail when I see the crowd in her house. Just a few friends, Priti had told me over the phone. Or had she said close friends? But this – it's a crush. I can't recognise anyone, nor does anyone show signs of recognising me, not even the few faces that look vaguely familiar. A couple of men who've moved to make room for me go on with their conversation. I'm forced to listen, there's no way I can move on, not unless I disturb them once again. In a while I gather that they're discussing the casting of a new TV serial. Of course, that's where I've seen them . . .

'Urmi!' It's Avinash. 'What are you doing here, skulking in a corner? Come inside, Priti has been looking for you.'

'And I'm trying to locate her.'

'She's around somewhere. Come on in.' He skilfully manoeuvres his way through the crowd. From the way he's going, it looks like he's leading me to some definite point, Priti perhaps. But when we get to the other end of the room, there's just the same kind of crowd, with clutches of people engrossed in earnest conversation. He stops and looks about helplessly, as if wondering what to do with me now he's got me here, and turns with unconcealed relief to a man who greets him. He introduces the man as just 'Shibu', he seems to presume the name means something to me.

'Let me get you something, what will you have?' he asks me and disappears, thankfully I imagine. We don't really

183

know each other, Avinash and I, but he's a kind man, he wouldn't have liked leaving me alone.

Now there's Shibu, we can entertain each other. I don't have to worry about what to say, for Shibu begins talking, he goes on rather, as if continuing a conversation we'd begun earlier. And from his talk I learn that he's a script-writer, that he has written the script for Priti's film which she's only just completed, and that this party is to celebrate the fact. He does not give me this information, it comes to me in the course of his talk. Obviously he presumes that I, as Priti's friend, know all these things. He looks surprised when I ask him abruptly 'What's the film about?'

'*Sati*,' he says. 'Actually, Priti had started on another idea, but somehow it wasn't working out. I don't know why, it was a good idea, really a very strong theme, you know. It was about a woman who's raped by her own husband . . .'

He tells me about it and I realise with horror that it is Mira's story, exaggerated, coloured, over-dramatised.

'We were struggling with it, when this happened. Priti's a great believer in Fate – I don't agree with her actually, but this time . . .'

A loud burst of laughter stops him. We look up to see Priti poised in the arch between the living and the dining room, a bowl held high over her head like an offering. There's mock applause, more laughter. Someone asks, 'Is that the Golden Lotus?' 'No, the Golden Bear' another voice retorts. 'Just garam garam samosas,' Priti replies laughing.

Avinash goes to her and I guess he's telling her about me, because her eyes travel over the room until they rest on me. She smiles, waves, thrusts the bowl into Avinash's hands and comes to me.

'Urmi, how wonderful you managed to come. I was just beginning to be afraid you wouldn't. I'd have been very angry if you'd stayed away. You know, Urmi, I heard you were involved in that case – the girl Kalpana . . .'

'I know her mother.'

She goes on to talk of Kalpana, she's full of it, she gloats over the fact that an investigation has been ordered . . .

'I think it's great that they could raise the issue in the Assembly, it just shows . . .'

'Victory for women, eh?'

'I should have guessed it would be you. Shibu, this is . . .'

'We've met. And talked.'

Her eyes flicker over us as if wondering what we've been talking about.

'Yes, Shibu, victory. Why not? The Chief Minister ate humble pie, didn't he? He apologised to the women for the violence the police used on them . . .'

'Victory nothing. It doesn't mean a thing. It's political. And as for apologising . . .'

'Priti, can I talk to you? No, not here, let's go in.'

She leads me into the bedroom with a trace of reluctance and closes the door, shutting out the party-noises.

'Priti, why didn't you tell me about the film?'

She hesitates. 'It all happened so fast, I can't believe even now that it's over. It was mad, the way we worked all of us, like we were possessed.'

She thinks I'm speaking of the film she's just completed. I should correct her, but I decide to let her have her say first.

'I was furious with you,' she says, with the frankness on which she always prides herself. 'And horribly depressed. When Baba fell ill I was low, so low, God, I was right down there. Then the woman who works for Baba came and told me about this girl in the next village. Her husband had just died, she said and they were going to make her a *sati*. I didn't believe her at first. *Sati?* In this day and age? What

185

about the police? But it was true. When I got there it was all over. As soon as I saw the crowds and felt the atmosphere – I can't describe it, it was eerie, I think we've got a touch of it in my film – it came to me. This is it, I told myself. I got in touch with Shibu immediately – luckily we think along the same lines, which is why we could get on with it that fast.'

'How is it?'

She pauses, seems to be considering. 'I don't know. I'm sort of blank. Some of them who've seen it say it's . . . well,' she smiles, 'great. I don't know. But certainly it's unusual and I don't mean just the theme or the techniques we've used . . .'

Priti is unstoppable today. It's her day. She is high, not on drink, she never drinks, but on achievement, praise, dreams of success, of awards at festivals. They're all heady stuff.

'I'm glad you've done it.'

'Are you?' She gives me a doubting look, sees I'm sincere and instantly responds to it. The awkwardness I've noticed in her and that slight suggestion of a pose fall off her.

'I've had a bad conscience about you.'

'If you mean that, you must do that script for me. I'd still like to do the film, I'm ready any time you say the word.'

The phone rings, letting me off having to reply. Priti picks it up. 'Hello, yes, that's right. Who? Urmi . . . Inniauntie, is that you?'

Inni? My heart begins knocking about in my chest, I feel breathless.

'Yes, she's right here . . .' She looks at me and, pushing me back into the chair, hands me the receiver. 'It's okay, Urmi, I'm sure it's nothing . . .'

'Urmi, the child Sandhya is here. She wants to talk to you.'

186

'Sandhya?'

'It's okay,' I mouth at Priti, responding to her inquiring look. She switches on the fan and goes out. The blast of air on my sweating body makes me feel suddenly chill. I shiver, pull my sari closely about me.

'Yes, Inni, put her on.'

There is silence. I can hear whispers, and it's Inni again.

'The poor child can't talk, she's in a state. She wants me to tell you her Sulumavshi is dead.'

'My God!'

'And her mother wants you. She sent the child to get you.'

'I'll be there, Inni. Tell Sandhya I'm leaving right away.'

I squeeze myself out of the place and am waiting for the lift when Priti comes running to me.

'Urmi, you're going. What is it?'

'Sorry, Priti, I should have told you. I have to go. A friend of mine – her sister's dead.'

'Oh no! I am sorry.'

The lift stops.

'I'm sorry too, going away like this.'

'Don't be silly, this isn't important. Would you like me to drop you home?'

'No, I'll get a taxi.'

'Keep in touch then.'

She puts a hand on my arm, closes the door and waves to me as the lift begins moving down. 'And Urmi,' her voice follows me, 'take care.'

The words knock about in the tiny enclosed space. 'Take care, take care, take care.'

The crowd in the room dissolves. I don't know how it happens – perhaps Sandhya sends them out, perhaps they go away thinking I'm a doctor. With both the door and the

187

window closed, it is dark, I can see nothing. Shakutai's voice guides me to her.

'Urmila . . .'

'I'm here.'

'She's gone, Urmila, she's gone.' I can see her face now. 'She killed herself. She poured a whole bottle of kerosene over herself and . . .'

She tries to raise her hand, but it falls back heavily by her side. The dreadful smell of kerosene seems to hang in the air. Or am I imagining it? No, it's real. Sandhya, conditioned to making tea for me each time I visit them, is lighting the stove.

'Sandhya, leave that alone, I don't want anything.'

She doesn't seem to have heard me. I go to her and try to stop her, but her eyes are as blank as her mother's. She does not seem to see me. Even when I put off the stove, she continues to sit there, crouching over it.

'Urmila, where are you?'

'I'm here.'

'Come here. I can't get up. My legs . . . And look at my hands,' she says, holding them out to me. They are cold and trembling. I take them between mine, chafe them. She lies still, her eyes closed.

'I brought her up with so much love, I wanted so much for her,' she murmurs.

'But why, Shakutai, why did she do it?'

'Her husband . . . Prabhakar, he . . . he did it to my Kalpana, my Sulu's husband . . . it was he . . .'

'Oh God!'

I know that the smell of kerosene will forever be to me the smell of pain, of betrayal, of death.

'I let her go home yesterday, I shouldn't have . . . why did I? But I didn't know, I never thought she would do this.'

She speaks with long pauses between words. And, as if that inner timing which had been part of her has deserted

188

her, the pauses, most of the time, coincide with the lull between trains, while she continues to speak when the trains go past. But her voice, a ghost of its former self, can no longer compete with the trains. I have to bend to catch her words; even so, I lose some of them.

'She was here last night. Yesterday it came in the papers that they had reopened the case. And he told her, "If the police ask you, tell them I was at home with you that whole evening and night." Then she knew. She came to me to tell me, to ask me what to do. What could I tell her, Urmila? I was angry with her. What can I tell you, I asked her. You should know what to do. And she went back home and . . . I never thought, I promise you, Urmila, I never thought she would do this. She finished her cooking, gave him his breakfast and then . . . The neighbours told me she was like a torch when she ran out, burning from head to toe, they said. My God, oh my God.'

She turns her head on the pillow, rolling it from side to side. And I know what it is she's trying to blank out. It's a vision of the woman aflame in the room with its TV set, its embroidered covers, its vases and dolls.

'When I went to the hospital, it was all over. They told me only this bit,' she shows me her palm, 'of her sari was left. That was all.'

She begins sobbing for the first time, a horribly agonised sobbing. Sandhya, who has crept to us, begins whimpering, 'Ai, don't, Ai-ga, Ai-ga . . .'

I can feel the child's body trembling. I put my arm about her; in a while, she is still. Shakutai too quietens down. For a moment there is silence in the room. Then Shakutai goes on.

'Sulu says he was always mad about Kalpana. Even then, when Kalpana went to live with them, he tried to . . . he wanted . . .' she gives up. 'She was only a child then, she was fourteen and he thought he could . . . That's why she

189

ran away and refused to go back. But she didn't tell me, why didn't she tell me? And where were my eyes? I should have known, I should have guessed. He used to look at her, he used to say things, he called her "My beauty", he used to praise her looks. I thought, he's her uncle, he's being affectionate. But Kalpana – I can remember how she used to walk out. And I used to scold her for that. I've done wrong, Urmila. I've done great wrong, such great wrong.'

'Shakutai, don't think of that now.'

'No, I have my whole life to think about it, all my life – God knows how many years. I have a fire burning inside me, here. Nothing can cool it, Urmila,' she cries out, 'nothing can cool it.' She holds my hand tight and it's only when she releases it and the blood flows back that I realise the pain.

After a long while, when I think she has fallen asleep, she says, 'She wanted to get married.'

'Who? Kalpana?'

'She told me, there was a boy she had come to know, she said they had fixed it up . . .'

'And?' I prompt her when she doesn't continue.

'I said, you can't. How could I let her? We didn't even know the boy's caste, leave alone his family. How could we hold our heads up among our people? But Kalpana was stubborn. I told Sulu about it, I thought maybe Kalpana would listen to Sulu. And Sulu told him that day, the day Kalpana was hurt. "Why did I tell him, Shakutai, why did I?" Sulu kept asking herself yesterday. After she told him about it, he went out, she said, and returned late, past midnight. He never used to tell her where he had been, but that night he sat with her, chatted with her, he told her he had gone to see a movie, he even told her which one, what it was about. And she thought, thank God, he's forgotten his anger. But the next morning, she found out he had

190

washed his own clothes, the first time he'd ever done such a thing. "You shouldn't have, why did you?" she asked. And he turned on her, he was so angry, it frightened her. And then, yesterday, when he said, "Tell the police I was at home" she knew.'

Someone is tapping at the door. Sandhya goes to open it. I can hear a low murmur of conversation. She returns, and in reply to my inquiring look, says 'A neighbour, she wanted Ai.' She looks helplessly at her mother as if expecting her to get up and take charge as usual, but Shakutai lies in a kind of stupor now. It is as if she had saved up all her energy to tell me these things; now she's done it, she's exhausted.

'Has she eaten anything today?' I ask Sandhya.

'I don't know.'

I try to rouse Shakutai to ask her, but she mumbles some words that have nothing to do with my question. She seems to have mixed up the two of them finally, Kalpana and her sister, Sulu. I don't know who it is she is talking about; perhaps, she doesn't either. Once she says Sandhya's name as well and I think of how beautiful they are, the names she has chosen for her daughters. Then I remember her telling me, 'It was my Sulu who chose names for my children, all three of them.'

After a while, she falls asleep, her mouth open. The room is steeped in silence, except when she snores a little. Suddenly she wakes up with a start. 'Sandhya,' she calls out wildly, 'Sandhya.'

'What is it, Ai?' The child panics at her mother's tone. 'I'm here, Ai, I'm here.'

Shakutai clutches the child in a frantic grip. Her eyes roll about, as if she is searching for something, then rest on my face. There is a desperate plea in them.

'Take her, Urmila, take her away with you. I can't look after her, I don't want her, I'll only destroy her like I did

191

Kalpana. Take her to your house, keep her there, I'm not fit to look after her.'

Shakutai is hysterical; she pushes the child away from her so violently that she falls down in a frightened heap. I try to soothe Shakutai.

'What's the matter with you, Shakutai? She's your daughter, she's going to stay here with you, you're her mother . . .'

'Ai, don't talk this way, why are you saying such things, what have I done . . .?'

'Sandhya, get a glass of water.'

When she is calmer, I say it again, 'Shakutai, Sandhya isn't going anywhere, she's staying here with you. You understand?'

Shakutai says nothing, just looks at me, her face despairing. She lies silent, breathing heavily. Her eyes keep moving to Sandhya – there is something fearful in that look.

'I'm not going anywhere, I want to be here, I want to stay here,' Sandhya sobs brokenly. In a while, exhausted by her emotions, she falls asleep. Her head sinks closer to her mother's body, once or twice she sits up with a jerk. Finally she is fast asleep, sprawling on the ground. I straighten her, push a pillow under her head, cover her scrawny body with a sheet.

The room is unbearably hot and sweltering, I can feel my clothes clinging damply to my body. Shakutai's immobility gives way to restlessness. She tosses, turns, sits up, lies down again, like a person tormented by an unbearable physical pain. I can see, I can feel her agony, but I can do nothing for her. I feel wretchedly, angrily helpless.

Shakutai talks to me through the night. It comes out in bits and pieces; often, she seems to be speaking to herself.

'Sulu was frightened, she was always frightened because she had no children. She was afraid he would throw her out, take another wife. And then she started getting these

192

white patches on her face, her arms, her neck. He stopped touching her after that. She told me this only yesterday, she kept everything to herself, she never told me her troubles, even about Kalpana – she knew, that first time, that he'd tried to put his hands on Kalpana. But she warned Kalpana not to tell me, not to tell anyone.'

It's when she stops speaking that I realise how absolute the silence now is. It's that brief time, between the end of one day and the beginning of another, when the city seems to pause, gathering its breath for the next surge of activity. The silence twangs in my ears.

'Get me Kalpana, he kept telling her, and you can stay on here, I don't mind. She came to me and I thought it was her idea, that's what she told me. I have no children, she said. If Kalpu marries him, she can be mistress of the house, she doesn't have to do anything, I'll do all the work, everything. I thought, what's wrong? At least he's not a drunkard, or a wife-beater or a waster like my husband. I thought, maybe this is the best thing for her . . .'

'You spoke to Kalpana?'

'Sulu did. And Kalpana . . .' She is silent again, for such a long time that I think she won't go on. 'Kalpana laughed. Sulu told me she laughed. You're mad, she said. Don't you know, she said, you can't have a second wife now? He can go to jail for it. Sulu begged her, she fell at her feet. It made me furious . . .' For the last time she flashes out in anger against Kalpana. 'How could she treat Sulu that way? Sulu loved her, she was like a mother to her, she was more a mother to her than I was. And what was wrong? He would have treated her like a queen, and my Sulu would have been there.'

'Shakutai, you know it would have been wrong.'

'Yes,' her voice comes out dull and lifeless. 'Yes, we were wrong, Sulu and I, we were both wrong.' She sighs.

'Anyway . . . Sulu told me he went crazy after that. He kept talking about Kalpana all the time, he could talk of nothing else. He used to go to her shop almost every evening. And then Kalpana said she was getting married . . . If only Sulu had had a child,' she says once. And again, 'What shall I do, Urmila? What shall I do?'

I realise this is not a cry of desperation. She is asking me for an answer, she wants me to tell her what she must do.

'Should I tell the police? What should I do?'

I know now why it is she wanted me here – not for comfort, not for consolation, no one can give her that, and there are enough women here to give her that kind of support anyway. No, it is for this that she wanted me here, to give her an answer to this question. She thinks I can give it to her. Can I?

It seems aeons before my lips can shape themselves to a reply. 'I can't tell you, Shakutai, you have to decide yourself.'

'What's the use now? Kalpana's destroyed, we destroyed her, Sulu and I. And now Sulu's gone also. What's the use of it, what's the use of anything?'

'You have Prakash and Sandhya . . .'

'No, Urmila, no!' she cries out wildly, 'I don't want any more of it, I've had enough, I've had enough, I've had enough . . .'

She goes on and on repeating the words until they finally fade away. I let her alone.

After a while, she speaks in a more normal tone. 'What a girl she was, Urmila, my Sulu, you should have seen her . . .'

I saw her once, I want to say, but I know it won't be true. The woman I saw, a woman who vanished with the rapidity of a frightened animal when she saw me, has nothing to do with this Sulu of Shakutai's. I only had a brief glimpse of her face, but it was enough to give me the reason for the pity in Shakutai's voice when she spoke of her sister.

'She is always doing something, she can't sit idle for a moment. You should see her home, Urmila, it is like a mirror, her floor, you can see your face in it. And all her vessels, they shine like silver. Once, before she got married, she pestered me to have a *Sankranti haldi-kumkum*. I didn't want to, I never had time for all those things, but she said she would do everything. She did it all so beautifully. She had embroidered a tablecloth for the table, and she arranged the *haldi-kumkum* things on it. She made little boxes of coloured paper to put the *tilgul* in, she got tiny mirrors and combs to give the women. They talked about it for days.' She lies still, as if savouring that memory. 'After marriage she changed. She was frightened, always frightened. What if he doesn't like this, what if he wants that, what if he is angry with me, what if he throws me out . . .? Nobody should live like that, Urmila, so full of fears. What kind of life is it? "I don't have your courage, Shakutai," she used to say to me. But was I born with this courage? I learnt, I had no choice, I had to have courage or stop living. But Sulu . . .'

Then she says, in a puzzled kind of way, 'Sulu's gone, but Kalpana . . .?'

The question hangs in the air between us. Neither of us speaks after that. Some time, sitting there, I fall asleep and dream I am in my own bed in Ranidurg. I try to get out and find my hands enmeshed in some soft material. It's the mosquito net, why has Baiajji put it up? I don't like it, I feel trapped . . .

I wake up to find myself sleeping on the chair. I wince with pain as I try to move, my neck is stiff. Someone, Shakutai of course, has covered me during the night with a soft, soap-smelling cotton sari, my hands are entangled in it.

'Are you awake?' Shakutai's voice comes to me. She is sitting by the stove, her face gaunt and shadowed under the unshaded bulb. I have to struggle out of the chair, even my body is stiff.

'You will have some tea?'

'Why are you up?'

'I've been up for hours. I had to fill the water, it comes only at night. And the men will need water for their baths.'

Yes, of course, they will be returning after Sulu's funeral.

'They should have come by now, they should have come long back, I can't understand why they haven't come yet.'

'Why didn't you wake me?'

'To fill the water? The neighbour women helped, we left all the pots and buckets outside, we didn't want to disturb you. Come and have your tea. Then you must go. Your mother and child will be waiting for you.'

Sandhya wakes up on hearing our voices. We are drinking our tea when someone taps at the door.

'Sandhya,' a voice calls.

'It's Baba.' Sandhya opens the door and clings to him. He pats her soothingly, but his eyes go to his wife.

'It's over?' she asks.

'Yes.'

For a moment she looks as if she's going to faint. Then she recovers herself and says, 'Have your bath, I have hot water ready for you. And where is Prakash?'

It seems surprising, when I come out of that room of grief and suffering, to find the world outside unchanged. After the darkness, the bright light hurts. I close my eyes for a moment as I stand in the doorless entrance, bracing myself to the ordeal of walking to the bus stop. A child, standing against the wall, gazing reflectively down at himself as he

196

shakes off the last few drops of urine, senses my presence and looks up at me. He seems startled to see me there. Possibly, it occurs to me, I look odd, dressed as I am in the colourful silk I'd worn for Priti's party; as incongruous, at this time and place, as the flamboyantly curved moustache someone has drawn on the simpering face of a heroine, on a movie poster behind the boy. He stares at me for a moment, makes a rude face and scampers away, flailing his arms in wide circles about him as he runs.

As if he has released me from a spell of stillness, I begin to move, willing my limbs into activity. There are still some huddled shapes on the pavement. As I walk past them, I think of Priti's mother, who ran over people like these, and of the hell she inhabited ever after. And then I think of Inni and Kartik, and of their anxiety about my absence from home all night. I prepare myself for questions, accusations, recriminations; but, to my surprise, Inni says nothing when she opens the door to me. It is I who ask, 'Where's Kartik?'

'Getting ready for his bath.'

And now, I think, as I let myself down thankfully into a chair, the questions will come. But Inni turns away saying, 'I have to get Kartik's breakfast ready.'

'Hasn't Rekha come?'

'Not yet. She's taking it easy these days. We'll have to talk to her.'

'Inni, I'll . . .'

Even as I get to my feet, the world goes black. I come back to find Inni and Kartik looking anxiously into my face.

'It's nothing. Just lack of food and sleep. Sleep more than food, actually.'

'You sit there, don't move. I'll get you some milk.'

Kartik brings the milk, balancing a brimming glass on a saucer with anxious solicitude. He stands by me while I take a sip, then asks, 'Is it nice, Mama?'

'Very nice.'

197

His rare smile lights up his face and he goes away leaving me there, nursing my glass of milk in my hands. And then, something happens to me. I can hear Kartik and Inni talking, I can hear the sounds of Kartik having his bath, Inni banging about in the kitchen. Familiar sounds, familiar voices. But, as if they've slipped away from me, all these things seem to be happening an immense distance away. So far that I can't reach them, I can never reach them. It's terrifying. The sensation of being shut out of their world is so strong that I have to force myself to sit still, not to thrash about wildly. In a while the panic dissolves; with an almost clinical detachment, I notice my heartbeats, my pulse, slowing down, coming back to normal.

The bell rings. I continue to sit there in some sort of a stupor while it rings again and again. Inni rushes out of the kitchen, sees me and gives me a surprised look.

'Urmi, you haven't had your milk!'

'No, I . . .'

'Drink it up and go and lie down for some time.'

Obediently I go into the bedroom and sit there, still with my glass in my hand. I can hear Rekha and Inni arguing, but the words mean nothing to me, they're just sounds. In a while, there is silence as the dust settles down on their quarrel. I doze off and wake up to Inni's voice. 'Urmi?'

I look at her blankly. She is dressed for her yoga.

'Are you all right?'

'I must have fallen asleep. Has Kartik gone?'

'Just five minutes back. He wanted to wake you . . .'

Her face is puzzled. She comes close to me, puts the back of her hand on my forehead, as if taking my temperature.

'I'm all right.'

'You shouldn't have gone, I never liked your getting involved with all this.'

'Let's not start that all over again, Inni.'

198

'I know, I can't say a thing to you,' she says resentfully.

'Anyway I have to go. Are you going to college?'

'Yes.'

'You don't look well.'

I don't reply. She goes away then, but suddenly at the door she turns and comes back.

'Urmi, I've been wanting to tell you something . . .'

Now what is it, I wonder wearily.

'Do you know why we – why your Papa sent you away to Ranidurg?'

It's such an odd thing to ask – whatever I'd expected her to say, it's not this.

'It was because I . . . because your Papa – he didn't trust me, he thought I couldn't . . . wouldn't look after you properly. I went out one day, I didn't leave you alone, I swear I didn't, Diwakar was there. Then Papa came home and found you crying and I wasn't at home. And he . . . oh my God, he was . . .'

I can see on her face the terror she had felt then, as if she has carried it within her all these years.

'I was frightened of you, Urmi,' it bursts out of her. 'I was too young, I was not prepared to have a child. And you were not easy, you used to cry all the time, I didn't know how to soothe you. Diwakar was good with you, he was better than me, but Papa said, "How could you leave her alone with a man!" Diwakar! He had been with us since I was a child, that's why Mummy sent him to help me, he was so gentle, but Papa said, "He's a man." Diwakar!'

The room seems full of the echoes of an old conflict – or am I imagining it? How could Inni ever have opposed Papa?

'Then he decided he would take you to his mother. He didn't say anything to me, he just took you away. I never imagined he wouldn't bring you back, I thought this was just to teach me a lesson, to punish me, but . . . I begged him, Urmi, I cried, I promised him I'd never leave you alone, but he wouldn't listen. Nothing could make him change his mind. You know your Papa . . . I didn't want you to be sent away to Ranidurg, believe me Urmi, I didn't want that, I wanted you with us, I never got used to the idea of your being in Ranidurg, I wanted you with me . . .'

There's something supplicatory about her; it's as if I'm seeing that girl-mother of long ago, kneeling before her husband for understanding, forgiveness. She wants me to give it to her, the absolution Papa never granted her.

I do. I put my arms round her, I tell her I believe her, that she never wanted me to be sent away. I say these things over and over again until she is calmer. She seems not only reassured, but unburdened, as if she's passed on her load to me. But I don't feel weighed down, either. It's something else. A sense of being vulnerable and naked, as if some armour I've been wearing all these years – against what? – has fallen off.

Inni seems to sense something, for she looks at me and says doubtfully, 'I shouldn't have told you, maybe. But just forget it now, Urmi, don't think of it again.'

'No, Inni, I won't.'

Then she is gone and I think of how I had agonised over why they had sent me away, I think of all the theories I had constructed and I begin to laugh – a laughter that suddenly turns into tears. It's a painful, agonising, tearing-my-insides-apart sobbing. My nose, my throat are blocked by great globs of mucus; it's the ugly, unrestrained crying of childhood. It goes on and on, my breath coming out in painful gasps. Rekha stops me finally. I hear her frightened voice, and with an effort I get hold of myself.

'Tai? What is it? Why are you crying?'

Why? Because the scars of an old cruelty have shown me how hopeless, how utterly hopeless it is? Because I've seen how bottomless the chasm is, how impossible to bridge? I can't say these things to Rekha. I wipe my face, blow my nose and try to smile at her.

'It's over, Rekha, it's all right now.'

'Have your bath,' she says. 'You'll feel better.'

She's right. There's something healing and reviving in the sharp, stinging needles of spray on my body. I let the water flow over me and it's like a benediction. I think of Baiajji pouring the last few mugs of water over my body, chanting the names of all the rivers as she did so. How I loved listening to the stately ring of the names when she chanted them!

To me, as a child, Baiajji was the fount of wisdom and love. But Inni says she could be cruel. You don't know her, she says. You don't know how she kept 'the other family' away from Aju – his own daughters!

Did Papa think so too? Is that why he persuaded Aju to give the money from the sale of Baiajji's orchards to those two half-sisters of his? A kind of expiation of his mother's unkindness, perhaps? But Papa himself, when I think of what he did to Inni, it frightens me. 'You know your Papa,' Inni said. I thought I did, I thought he was a just man, a wise man, but Inni was wiser. She knows what mattered was that Diwakar was 'gentle and good'. I thought Papa loved Inni deeply, yet . . .

No, it's true, he did love Inni. Why do I imagine that love absolves us from being cruel? There's Shakutai – she says she loves her daughter; but I know, and she does too, that she was cruel to her.

Perhaps it is this, the divide in ourselves, that is the great divide. Perhaps it's this divide in ourselves that's the hardest to bridge, the hardest to accept, to live with.

'What shall I do, Urmila?' Shakutai asked me. Was she saying, 'How do I go on?', knowing what I do about myself? Did Priti's mother too ask herself this question? And did

201

she then retreat into madness because she realised there's no answer?

The bleak thought saddens me. I try to get out of it by thinking of the awesome courage of the few who tried to find an answer. But what use have they been to us? Detachment, love, brotherhood, non-violence – they're just words. They mean nothing to our living. *Dharma, Dharma, Dharma*, the *Mahabharata* endlessly, tirelessly repeats. Yet at the end, the poet cries out in despair, 'I raise my arms and I shout, but no one listens.'

'Feeling better?' Rekha asks me when I come out. She doesn't wait for my reply, but I notice she's got everything ready for me in the kitchen today. Tomorrow, my distress forgotten, she'll be back to her whimsical, argumentative self, but today . . .

'Ayya,' she screams, 'I quite forgot. There were two phone calls. One from Vanaatai and one from Bhaskar doctor. Vanaatai said she will come here in the evening. And the doctor said you must phone him when you have time.'

Bhaskar? Why has he . . .? Can I ring him now? I look at the time and regretfully decide I can't. But the fact that he rang me up is somehow comforting.

'Rekha, have you kneaded the chappati dough?'

'Yes, tai.'

And so we go on. 'I don't want any more, I've had enough, I've had enough,' Shakutai cried out. But in the morning I found her getting on with her chores. You can never opt out, you can never lay it down, the burden of belonging to the human race. There's only one way out of this *Chakravyuha*. Abhimanyu had to die, there was no other way he could have got out.

And, now that I think of it, I remember a kind of resoluteness in Shakutai as she sat before the stove in the morning. She looked as if she had come to some kind of a decision. 'Sulu's dead, but Kalpana . . .?' she asked herself. I have a feeling Shakutai knows it now, that her daughter's tragedy, her sister's death can no longer be shrouded in silence. Or is this wishful thinking on my part? If Shakutai has made up her mind, it lets me off the terrible task of answering her question, 'What shall I do?' Yet if she does ask, I can no longer avoid giving her an answer. The thought of all that lies ahead oppresses me, but I can see no road that can take us back. That's no longer possible.

'Tai . . .,' Rekha's impatient voice calls out, 'what vegetables do you want me to wash?'

'I'm coming, Rekha, in a minute.'

I race through my chores in the next one hour – cooking, getting ready for college, looking through my timetable, my notes, preparing Kartik's lunchbox. This is how life is for most of us, most of the time; we are absorbed in the daily routine of living. The main urge is always to survive. Mira realised that.

> Just as the utter futility of living overwhelms me, I am terrified by the thought of dying, of ceasing to be.

But what terrible things we do in the process of surviving. And yet, I think of Vanaa, heavily pregnant, sitting by me, holding my hand during the pains before Kartik was born, I remember Kishore's face when he first saw Anu, I think of Akka crying for Mira, of Inni's grief when Papa told her about his illness, of Papa's anguished face watching her, of the touch of grace there was in Shakutai's hand when she covered me gently at night while I slept, of the love with which she speaks of her sister, of Sandhya . . .

Is this it, 'the spring of life' Mira was looking for?

GLOSSARY

Ai – mother

Ajji – grandmother

Aju – diminutive of ajja, grandfather

Appa, Baba – father

Bala – child

Bhaskar and Jyoti – Bhaskar is the sun and Jyoti means light

Blade of grass – Sita, wife of Rama, the hero of the epic *Ramayana*, was abducted by Ravana. During the period of her stay in his palace, the virtuous Sita kept Ravana at bay with the help of a blade of grass which she kept between them

Chaitra-Gouri puja – a religious ritual, performed by women during the first month of the Hindu calendar (Chaitra)

Chakravyuha – a battle formation mentioned in the *Mahabharata*. Young Abhimanyu, son of the hero Arjuna, who had been taught by his father the secret of penetrating it, bravely entered the formation, but not knowing how to get out was hacked to death inside it by the Kauravas

Chamchi – sycophant, tell-tale. A word of slang

Chawl – tenement of one-room homes

Didi, Tai – elder sister. Also used as term of respect

Dilliwali – the person (feminine here) from Delhi

Ek Kalpanéchi katha – Kalpana means imagination. Therefore it could be either Kalpana's story or an imagined story

Ghanshyam – name of the god Krishna, also means dark

Haldi-kumkum ceremony – religious rituals which are also social occasions for women, in which haldi (turmeric) and kumkum, flowers, fruits, attar etc., are offered to women

IAS – Indian Administrative Service

Kaajal – eye-black, collyrium

205

Kaka – uncle, literally father's brother

Kalidasa – Sanskrit poet and dramatist. Shakuntala and Dushyanta are two characters in his most famous and loved drama *Abhijnana Shakuntala*

Karna's armour – Karna, the illegitimate son of Kunti, the mother of the Pandava brothers in the *Mahabharata*, was born with a divine armour which made him invincible. His famed generosity, however, made him gift it to Indra who, in the disguise of a Brahmin, asked him for it

Kumkum – red mark on a Hindu woman's forehead. Widows are not supposed to wear it

Laxmi Narayan – the god Vishnu and his spouse Laxmi, supposedly the ideal couple

Mama – uncle, literally mother's brother

Mangalsutra – black beads worn by a married woman whose husband is living

Matka – a kind of gambling, common in Bombay

Mavshi – aunt, literally mother's sister

Meera bhajan – a devotional song composed by the saint-poet Meera

Morcha – demonstration

Paan – betel leaf: the leaf is eaten along with the betel nut, lime, optionally other spices, and for the hardened, tobacco

Paperwalas – journalists

Pranaayaam – a part of yoga, to do with breath control

Raaga – series of notes upon which a melody is based

Rangoli – designs drawn in white and coloured powder

Renamed her Nirmala – even the first name of a woman is changed after marriage among some communities. This is done ritually by the husband tracing the new name on rice in a ceremony when the bride enters her new home

Sakhi – friend, companion

Sankranti – a festival. **Tilgul** is a sweet specially prepared on this day

Siva and his nodding Bull – all the gods in the Hindu pantheon have their own vehicles. The bull is Siva's

S T bus stand – the government-owned bus terminal

Three long days – women used to be set apart for the first three days of their menstruation as unclean

Upanisads – mystical texts, part of the Vedic literature of ancient India

Waheeda (Rehman) – a movie actress